DIAMONDS ARE A COWGIRL'S BEST FRIEND

Other books by Suzanne Walter:

To Catch a Cowgirl

DIAMONDS ARE A COWGIRL'S BEST FRIEND

•

Suzanne Walter

AVALON BOOKS
NEW YORK

Wal

This book is dedicated to the RT Women's Group.
You are my friends, my critique partners,
and the best support system I could ever hope for.

I would also like to dedicate this book to
those who bought the first one. I would be a
writer without you, but its nice to know that
someone wants to read what I've created.

Finally, I would like to thank my editors; Erin for
being so easy to talk to and Abby for loving my book
(and not just because my heroine shares her name).

Prologue

Balesworth Morning Review
Sunday Morning Edition

DYMOND GALA, "MOTHER OF ALL PARTIES"

By the time you read this, the leftover champagne will be flat, the violinist will have replaced three broken strings, and this hardworking gossip hound will have collapsed into bed with a couple of aspirin and caviar on her breath. It was the premier social event of the season, darlings. And if I didn't see you there then I guess you really are a nobody, because all the who's who of Balesworth were invited.

The party was held to welcome Percival Chase Dymond IV home after an eight-year stay in New York. Rumor has it he'll be taking over Dymond Enterprises, though I have yet to confirm that delicious detail with the family. The highlight of the evening was the surprise announcement made by Percival's father. It seems the Diamond Boy might soon be getting engaged to the gorgeous Georgia Tiessen, a wealthy socialite whose family hails from Texas. It makes me want to cry thinking some lucky girl stole such a tasty piece of meat away before I could sink my red-lacquered fingernails into him.

Perhaps I'll find a juicy man of my own at one of this spring's numerous social events . . .

Chapter One

"**O**h my God!" Panic squeezed Abigail Blue's vocal cords into a tight squeak. "I think I killed him."

The phone rang. Abby snatched the receiver off the wall and put it to her ear. "Oh my God, oh my God, oh my God."

"What?" The voice on the other end of the phone shouted at her. "What's going on?" It was Julia Kidd, Abby's best friend and official crisis counselor. Of course, this was a more serious disaster than what shoes to wear on a date with Lewis, the bee-keeping locksmith. "Abby? Is that you? Are you there?"

Abby stretched the phone cord to its limit so she could look at the prone form on her barn floor. He was such a big man; how had she knocked him out with just one hit? His chest still rose and fell in a steady rhythm; she hadn't killed him . . . yet.

"I should call an ambulance," she mumbled, mangling the cord in her fingers. "This guy could have a concussion, or his brain could be hemorrhaging." She was wasting precious time. "Wait . . . doesn't a person bleed from the ear, or the mouth, or the nose, or something when he's hemorrhaged?"

"*What* the heck is going on?" Julia pressed.

"I gotta go."

"No! Wait! Check out his face, see if there is any blood."

"Okay . . . hold on." Abby dropped the receiver and knelt down beside him. Her hand shook as she reached out to touch his face. She clenched her fist to steady her nerves, then wrapped her fingers around his strong jaw to tilt his face toward her—no blood. She ran her free hand through his sandy-brown hair for unseen injuries—nothing, aside from the lump on his temple where she had hit him. His Roman nose looked like it might have been broken once—thankfully not by her.

"Abby? Abby!" Julia was still on the phone.

She got up off the barn floor and picked up the phone. "Yes?"

"I thought you hung up! What's going on? What happened?"

"I was brushing Aurora." The mare stood patiently on the cross-ties, not at all frazzled by the man lying on the floor in front of her. "This man stumbled out of one of the stalls and he was huge and I was scared so I screamed and then I hit him," she babbled.

"With your fist?"

"No." Abby shook her head regardless of the fact that her friend couldn't see it. "A brush." The man groaned at her statement and shifted, but remained unconscious.

Couldn't people in comas hear what was being said even though they didn't respond? Abby's stomach lurched at the thought. "You know the red and white one with the soft bristles and the wooden back?"

"Yeah."

"I hit him with the hard side."

"Oh no."

"I caught him across his right temple," Abby continued.

"Oh, that's bad."

"Tell me about it." She bit her lip. The man still showed no sign of alertness. She moved closer and nudged his shoe. He didn't respond. "He just crumpled to the floor like I shot him. His eyes rolled back in his head and everything. It was horrible!"

Abby stared hard at the stranger. Something tickled her memory. She stretched the cord to its limit and gasped. His face was the same one she had seen in the morning newspaper. "Oh, no!"

"What?" Julia's voice rose.

Abby gazed at the face she'd seen on the social page. She wished she'd recognized him sooner—like before she'd knocked him out. Her stomach turned. "I can't believe this! Why me?"

"What is it? What's wrong *now?*" Julia ordered.

"Well . . ." she took a deep breath before blurting, "He's kind of an *important* person."

"Abby, Shady Blue Stables is my investment too. I'm your head jockey. Who is this important person?"

"A Dymond."

"*Dymond?* As in, Percival-Dymond-the-Third-hates-you-because-you-refused-to-train-his-horses, Dymond?" Julia's voice broke. "How *could* you?"

"It wasn't like I got up this morning and the first thing on my agenda was to knock off some rich guy," Abby protested. "He scared the tar out of me. I just reacted."

The man groaned and she leaned forward to look at his face.

"Which he?" Julia probed.

"Percival Chase Dymond the *Fourth*."

"Oh good glory, Percy Jr. You knocked out the *Diamond Boy?*"

"The one and only." The press had given him the title "Diamond Boy" to separate him from his father when they were reporting a juicy piece of gossip on the social page. Unfortunately for him, the name had stuck.

"Don't call me Percival," the man slurred. His voice was like sandpaper—the final result of a very hard night, or a very good one. How had he ended up in her barn?

Abby watched as his body returned to life. A few pieces of hay clung to his hair. It looked like he had been sleeping in the stall.

"Don't call me Percy . . ." He squinted up at her, holding his forehead like any movement would cause it to split apart.

His eyes were slate gray, the same color as Aurora's dapples.

"And if you call me Junior . . ." he grimaced. "I think I'm going to be sick."

"I gotta go," Abby said. "He's coming to and he sounds delirious."

"Not delirious." He squeezed his eyes shut. "I *really* think I'm gonna be sick."

"Julia, I have to go. He's going to be sick!" *And I just swept*, she thought as she hung up the phone and knelt down beside the man again. She should get him up, or at least to his side, so he wouldn't choke. *Good grief, he's a giant! How am I supposed to move him?*

"Mr. Dymond? Sir?" She shook him a little and tried to get him to respond. When he didn't, she started to panic and shook him harder. "Hey, buddy! I need some help here. You've got to get up."

Please, please don't let him pass out again. "Come on, stay with me," she urged.

She slid her hands under one massive shoulder and struggled to move the man, but his large frame proved to be a dead weight, and the fine material of his rumpled suit jacket covering hard muscle made for a slippery hold.

What would he look like under all of his clothing? An image of bronzed skin, rippling muscles and an expansive chest sprung up in her mind. She snatched her hands back and rocked onto her heels. *Why is this guy affecting me like this*?

He groaned again. She wished the article she had read on the party had mentioned that the Diamond Boy would be sleeping in her barn overnight. She could have used the warning—it would have given her a chance to prepare herself against the onslaught of hormones his body was causing.

"Help me up, will you?" he groused, making no attempt to help himself.

"Ugh." Abby couldn't stop the reaction as his breath wafted over her. She fought back the stale smell of alcohol as it combined with the sharp scent of hay and horses and stole into her nostrils. It made her want to gag. "You're drunk. Why don't you tell me what you're doing in my barn, instead of giving me a hard time?"

"I am lying on the floor," he announced solemnly and slowly.

A smile twitched at her lips. She wasn't going to get a straight answer from him in this condition. She had to get him out of the barn. Grabbing his arm, she slung it over his chest for leverage, then threw her shoulder into his.

He started to move. Her running shoes grated against the floor as they slid on the concrete. She was no lightweight, but as she tried to roll him over she broke into a sweat.

"Anyone ever tell you, you have real nice lips?" he asked. "Kissing lips. That's what I would call them."

Abby's feet slid out from under her, sending her sprawling across his chest. The feeling was electric. She quickly pushed herself off and up onto her feet. "This isn't going to work."

He held both his arms out to her. "Why don't I pull you up?"

This time a full smile crept onto her lips. Drunk or not, he was still pretty cute. *And practically engaged*, she reminded herself. "I'm already up. It's you who needs to get to your feet."

"Mmmmm, okay." He lowered his hands and rested them on his chest. "Why don't you come down here with me?"

Why me? Why is one of Balesworth's most powerful men lying on my floor? And why does he have to be so darn sexy? "As great as your offer sounds, Mr. Dymond, I have to get you home."

"If you say so." He struggled to get to his feet, teetering to and fro as he rose. Almost standing, he pitched forward into Abby's arms and sent them both reeling backwards. His hard chest crushed her against the rough, wooden, barn wall.

Everywhere his body touched hers she felt warm; from

his hands gripping her arms, to his legs straddling hers. She squeezed her eyes shut and silently begged him to get off her before she did something stupid like kiss him with the lips he seemed to like so much.

"There!"

Her eyes opened to see him beaming at her.

"I did it," he said.

You certainly did, Abby thought. *But what are you doing to me?*

She stepped forward and slung his arm across her shoulders as he started to wobble. "Let's get you up to the house before you fall down again." They wove out of the barn and across the driveway, his weight making it difficult for her to support and steer him toward her door.

"Nice house," he said, as they staggered up the back steps. "Little."

"We can't *all* live in mansions," Abby retorted, her pride stung. "And some of us like living in small houses—saves the cost of hiring a maid." She shouldn't be so defensive. The man wasn't trying to insult her. He was drunk. Martin, her ex-husband, would have hated the place, but she lived alone now and spent most of her free time in the barn.

After an awkward struggle she managed to get him through the door into the kitchen and onto one of the stools. "I'll call your place and see if there's someone who can pick you up."

"I'd be happier if you let *me* pick *you* up." He gave her a lopsided leer.

Oh brother. He was sexy, drunk and probably dumb as a post too, judging by his dialogue. She'd have to spell it out to him. "I need your phone number."

"No you don't, sugar. I'm right here."

Yup, woodpeckers would have hunting season on him. Some guys were blessed with money, looks *and* brains, but two out of three wasn't bad. "I need your number so I can get someone to take you home."

"Rather stay here. Georgia's at my house." He wrinkled

his nose. "She calls me Percy." His voice rose into a high falsetto. "Percy, darling, I'm going to the hair dresser. Percy, be a dear and fetch my compact. Percy, I broke a nail! Whatever shall I do?" He pursed his lips into the perfect diva pout.

Abby laughed. So being rich had its downfalls, too. "If you don't like being Percy, what *do* you want to be called?"

"Chase. All my friends call me Chase."

Abby thought about introducing herself, but when she considered the fact that she didn't get along with his father, she figured it would be better to leave her name out of the conversation. "Well, Chase, we better get you home before Georgia has another crisis. Whatever will she do without you?"

He shook his head. "Can't go home."

"Why not?" she asked.

"Don't remember my phone number."

"Good grief," she sighed. "I'm going to have to take you there myself. But first we have to do something about your eye." His right eye was already beginning to bruise and swell.

"What's wrong with it?" Chase asked. "Don't you like the color?" He frowned. "I have two . . . both the same. I'd have to change them both."

She stifled a grin. "Their color's fine." In fact, better than fine. "But, I think you're going to have one terrific shiner."

"Well . . . how did that happen?" He touched the side of his face and winced.

"Don't you remember?" Abby couldn't believe her luck. Maybe she wouldn't get sued out of farm and home, and have to live in a cardboard box.

"Remember what?"

"You got hit," she said evasively.

"When?"

Abby stared at him. "Maybe it happened at the party last night." She turned toward her refrigerator so he wouldn't see the hot flush that flooded her cheeks when she told a fib.

"No . . ." he said from his seat behind her. "That's not it."

She opened the refrigerator door and tried to ignore the guilt. No ice. Her hand went to the steak. It was the steak she had bought the day before when Canon Ball won his claiming race. She was going to have it for a celebratory dinner. She shrugged and reached for it. Black eyes were always treated with steak in the movies. He really did deserve her dinner, since she was the one who'd clobbered him.

Abby sighed and lifted the plate out of the refrigerator. *Bye-bye, filet mignon. Hello, macaroni and cheese.* She set the plate on the counter and unwrapped the brown paper packaging. Chase mumbled something about being hit. The soft rumble of his voice made her heart race. She tried her best to ignore the reaction he caused.

"Close your eyes and tilt your head back," she urged.

Chase did as he was told and she laid the steak across his face, then grabbed his hand to hold it on. Another sharp zing rushed up her arm when she touched him. It was unnerving. She told herself it was just the weather. There was probably an electrical storm moving into the area.

"I have to go into the barn and put Aurora in her stall before we leave."

"Okay." Chase lifted the corner of the steak up and peeked at her. "You wan' any help?" The slurred question was followed by a slight wobble on the chair.

"No!" She thrust out her hand. "You stay here! You're too heavy for me to lift off the floor if you fall down again. I won't be long." She escaped out the door before he could follow her.

Abby quickly returned Aurora to her stall, checked the barn, and jogged back to the house. When she opened up the backdoor and stepped into her kitchen, her guest lifted the steak from his face and glared at her.

"*You* hit me!"

Busted. "Are you sure?" she asked, hoping the alcohol he'd consumed the night before had numbed his brain enough that he'd forget again.

"No. I mean yes. It was *you*. You're the one who hit me."

Maybe she could confuse the issue. "With what?"

"A brush," he said, "I'm certain. I saw it right before it smacked me."

She stifled a giggle. This was not funny. This was serious. "You're right," she confessed. "I'm sorry."

"S'all right." Chase grinned at her. "For a kiss I'll forgive you."

It would be as easy to do as laying a bet with a crooked bookie—and about as wise. "How about I give you a ride home instead of making you walk?" she offered. She pulled a tattered, blue and silver Dallas Cowboys cap off its peg, tugged her hair through the hole in the back and prayed Percy Sr. wouldn't recognize her when she dropped his son off.

"Okay." Chase stood a little steadier this time when he got off the stool. "But I'd rather have a kiss."

Me too, but we'd both regret it when you sober up. Abby braced his body again with her own. He leaned into her as he clutched the steak to the right side of his face. She could barely support his weight and her knees threatened to buckle as they stumbled out the door to her truck. When they got there she propped him against it as she opened the door. She guided him inside and tried not to touch him while she reached across his lap to fasten the seat belt.

With Chase secured in the passenger seat, she closed the door and ran her fingers across the "Shady Blue Stables" silver lettering on the blue panel. She made her way around the vehicle praying; *please don't be sick in my car.*

Abby slid inside and started the engine. Her passenger flopped his head against the back of the seat. "Are you going to be okay?" she asked.

"Mhmmph," was his only reply.

She drove to Chase's farm as quickly as she could. The ride was silent; her nerves stretched tighter and tighter with each passing mile. An imposing black metal gate slid open when she pulled up in front of his drive. "Thank goodness there's no intercom to explain myself into." She glanced at her quiet passenger as they wound up the long paved driveway. "You never told me how you ended up at my farm."

"Cab," he grunted.

He was going to have one heck of a hangover and she didn't want to be around to witness it. Abby bet talking hurt. She had made the mistake of drinking too much only once in her life and had vowed the next day to never do it again. Waking up with her face stuck to the floor and a knot in her stomach that felt like a wild pony trying to kick her way out was not something she wanted to repeat.

"Why did you sleep in my barn instead of trying the house?" Abby asked.

"Don't know," he shrugged. "Guess I was trying to avoid the 'wrath of Georgia.' Her tongue is almost as sharp as her nails."

Abby smiled as she turned into the paved circle in front of the grand house. White pillars graced an entrance that could have easily doubled for city hall. An immaculate rose garden framed the stone walls of the structure. She parked her truck away from the door, effectively hiding the name on the side panels.

What do three people do with a place this size? she wondered as she got out, staring at the sprawling monstrosity.

"You're home," she announced, helping Chase out of the truck.

Abby thought for a moment about ringing the bell and then running to her truck and leaving, but Chase would probably fall over and, with her luck, break his leg. When she finally got up the courage to press the doorbell, it gonged rather than rang.

The door swung open. A small, slim, well-dressed man who had to be the butler eyed Abby and her companion. "May I . . ." His gaze cut to Chase. "Are you all right, sir?" he asked, looking perplexed. "What happened?"

"I brought Mr. Dymond home."

The butler looked at her.

"I found him sleeping in my barn this morning."

"Oh?" He arched an eyebrow.

"It's not like that!" she sputtered. "Nothing else happened, I swear." She felt her cheeks grow hot.

Chase pulled the steak away from his face. "It's the truth, Roger. I *only* slept in her barn." He glanced around. "Where're my parents?"

"Right here." A petite, blonde woman rushed to the doorway and gaped. "My goodness! What happened?"

Chase groaned and slapped the steak back over his eye. "I got hit."

Abby pulled her hat low and studied her scuffed boots. If she was lucky, Chase's father wouldn't come to the door. She wasn't lucky.

"What's Junior gotten himself into now?" Percy Dymond was a large, dark-haired man. She could see where Chase got his height.

"He's been hit, dear." The fair-haired woman turned back to her son. "*What* is on your face?" Her pert nose wrinkled.

"Steak. For the swelling."

"It's disgusting!" his mother replied. "Roger,take it away and get an ice pack for Junior."

"Yes, ma'am." The butler held out his hand and let Chase drop the steak into it. Abby had to give the man credit; he never once dropped his dignified expression. She would have had a hard time keeping her composure in his position.

"You . . . Miss . . ." The woman looked at Abby. "What do you know about this?" She waved in the general direction of her son.

"I—" *Bye-bye, farm. Bye-bye, truck.* Maybe Julia and her husband would let her sleep on their floor. "I—"

"Found me in her barn," Chase supplied. "She didn't know how I got there."

A flurry of blonde curls and pink-glossed lips pushed her way through the doorway and launched herself at Chase. "Percy, baby," she crooned. "*Where* have you been? We were *so* worried about you."

The woman was perfect and petite; she made Abby feel

like a rangy foal. In fact, both of the women made her feel awkward. She could look good when she wanted to, but to be polished all the time was an art unto itself. Abby would rather be in the barn.

Chase attempted to fend off the blonde's advances. "I'm fine. Really."

"Who did this to you?" Georgia Tiessen pulled back and her gaze zeroed in on Abby. "Was it her?"

"No . . . in a fight." Chase gave Abby a meaningful look.

She realized he was covering for her. For the first time that morning, his gaze was sober and assessing.

"Cab dropped me off at the wrong farm." He smiled briefly at Abby. "Thanks for driving me and stuff."

"But, baby . . ." Georgia fastened her hands onto Chase's jacket lapels, successfully drawing his attention back to her. "*Who* hit you?"

He put his hand to his head and feigned deep thought. "It was these two guys . . . they were making fun of your shoes . . . something about them not matching your dress."

"Ooh!" Georgia squealed, making Chase flinch.

"And you defended my honor, Percy?" She gave him a big, resounding kiss. "That's so sweet! Let me get you inside and take care of your battle wounds."

"It wasn't much of a battle." He let her drag him through the door. "I got hit and I went down."

"Oh, but there must be *something* I can do to make it better."

"I'm sure a kiss would cure me," Chase answered, but he was looking over his shoulder at Abby. He made an unsuccessful attempt at a wink, which was more obvious than subtle. Even such a pathetic effort had her sizzling from her toes to her hair, and she was sure the others must have felt the heat rising off her before he turned and disappeared into the house.

His parents stood stiffly in the doorway.

"We can't thank you enough for bringing Junior home."

Mr. Dymond shook Abby's hand firmly. "I have the strangest feeling I know you from somewhere, Miss . . ."

"Leave the poor girl alone, Percy." Mrs. Dymond broke in. "I'm sure she has somewhere she has to be."

Abby smiled, grateful for the chance to escape. "I should get back home."

"Yes, dear," Mrs. Dymond said. "And thanks for the . . . steak." She half smiled and stepped back to let her husband close the door. Abby could hear her exclaim from the other side, "For goodness sakes, Percy! You don't know *her*! We don't associate with her sort!"

Abby stared at the ornamental brass knocker for a moment, then turned to leave. She should have been insulted, but instead, all she felt was relief. She climbed back into the truck and thanked her lucky stars things had turned out as well as they did. For starters, Percy Dymond didn't realize who she was. Secondly, Chase was okay. Besides a killer hangover and some bad bruising, he would walk away from the experience unscathed. So would she, if he kept to his fight story.

Abby suspected Georgia would give him worse than a black eye if she found out how flirtatious he had been. Georgia was a barracuda—not the innocent, defenseless, woman she acted like. It was clear she could take care of herself, and sorry was the person who got in her way.

Not that Abby planned to get in the way. Chase was exactly the kind of trouble she didn't need. The best thing she could do was forget she ever met him.

Chapter Two

Chase woke up later that day with a monstrous hangover. He was quite sure death would be a better option. A stampede raged through his head and his stomach protested every tiny hoofbeat. He cracked open an eyelid and snapped it shut again.

"Oohhh . . ." he croaked. "Not a good idea." Adding the sense of sight to everything else only made him queasier. How was he going to make it into the bathroom without moving?

His stomach wasn't going to wait for the answer. He made a dash for the adjoining room and tried to ignore his pounding head. This wasn't turning into the ideal morning.

It had been stupid to try to out-drink Theodore Jamison. The man was a camel when it came to alcohol. He was obviously storing up for a dry spell. Not that he could blame Theo for the hangover. It was his own fault. He was depressed about leaving a lifestyle he loved in New York to save a family business he had desperately tried to escape. That, coupled with his shock over his father's announcement of a pending engagement between him and Georgia, had sent him straight into a drunken stupor.

Was it only two weeks ago that he had been planning to come for his best friend, Al Taylor's wedding? Had he known then that the trip would morph into a permanent stay, and that Georgia was planning on trapping him into marriage, he might have booked a ticket for the farthest reaches of Siberia rather than Kentucky.

Chase sat up on the tiled floor of the bathroom. It was an enormous room. He didn't know why his parents needed such a large house. Maybe they hoped to fill it with grandkids.

"Oh no, Georgia's children."

He stopped staring at his blurry reflection in the tile of the bathtub wall and pushed himself off the floor and over to the shower. He reached in the glass doors and turned on the water, then shed the clothes he was still wearing from the previous night and threw them in the hamper. It might have been better to burn them.

Warm water massaged his aching muscles when he stepped into the shower, but it didn't help his head any. The spray washed in waves of recollections from his heated dreams.

Intense, deep blue eyes haunted him. A wide smile begged for a kiss. Long, long legs wrapped in course denim teased at his memory. A face formed in his mind. She had straight, dark brown hair that cascaded down her back. Without a doubt she was the most beautiful girl Chase had ever dreamed up.

He got out of the shower and toweled off. When he walked to the mirror and saw his swollen, black eye, realization finally dawned. The woman was real. He remembered the barn now and how she had knocked him out. The smell of raw steak was still distinct in his nostrils, which wasn't helping his stomach any. He also remembered telling his parents he was in a brawl. Why couldn't he think of his fantasy woman's name?

He shaved and dressed before easing himself downstairs. The hall clock chimed eleven. One of his father's horses was running that afternoon and Chase was expected to be at the racetrack.

Roger waited for him at the foot of the stairs with a glass of orange juice and a bottle of extra strength aspirin. "Morning, sir." The butler held out the contents of his serving tray. "Breakfast?"

Chase grabbed for the aspirin and swallowed two with the juice before he spoke. "You must have read my mind, Roger. If you showed up with a plate full of eggs and bacon I'd be running for the bathroom."

"That's why they call it a hangover, sir." He quirked a slight smile before continuing, "You hang over the toilet and expel your sins from the previous night."

"Don't remind me. I don't think my family will ever forgive me for the way I behaved last night. It will be a permanent black mark on my parents' social record," Chase said sarcastically. He ran a hand through his still-damp locks. "Nevermind Georgia. Why do I keep forgetting about her and her feelings?"

"As your butler, I'd say perhaps the relationship is still too new. As your friend, I wonder if you'll ever get used to Miss Georgia."

Chase cringed. "She's really not so bad," he stated more for his own benefit. "She's pretty, she educated and she's wealthy. What more could I ask for?"

"How about a woman who raises your temperature above the thermometer reading on a grocery store freezer?" Roger asked.

"I'm attracted to her . . . kinda."

"Lukewarm fuzzy feelings aren't the degree of passion I was thinking about." The butler quirked an eyebrow at him. "I think the woman a man is with should be special enough that he would risk everything to defend her. Maybe even act like a fool in front of his family for her."

"If you're talking about the woman who dropped me off this morning, forget it," Chase said. "For starters, I was still fairly drunk and not thinking clearly. I don't even know her name."

"Mmmmm . . . guess I was wrong then. I could have

sworn you were attracted to her. You couldn't stop staring at her."

He hoped everyone didn't find him so obvious, especially since he was supposed to be dating Georgia. It was time he had a talk with her. "Is Georgia still here, or did she go to the track with my parents?"

"She's waiting for you in the library, sir. I suspect she's halfway through her stack of fashion magazines by now."

"I should get going. I've kept her waiting long enough." He walked down the cavernous hallway.

"I did a little investigating and found out the lady's name is Abigail Blue."

Chase stopped and looked back. "How'd you find out her name?"

Roger shrugged. "I have a friend on the police force who owes me a favor. I had him look up her license plate. You might also be interested to know that she works at the racetrack."

"Thanks, Roger." He smiled at the butler and left to find his girlfriend.

"Percy, darling," Georgia simpered sweetly, as they drove through the gates of Balesworth Downs, the thoroughbred racetrack ten miles out of town. "All I'm asking is whether she's a friend of yours."

Chase gritted his teeth, clenched the steering wheel of his car, and stared at the road through his dark sunglasses. They'd been over this same question five times since he'd entered the library at home. Each time Georgia asked a little nicer, a sure sign of just how mad she really was.

He had discovered a short time ago that her perfectly polished manners improved as she became closer to losing control—not that he ever expected she would. Georgia was far too well bred to do something as common as throwing a hissy fit. Even if it would make her a little more appealing to him. At least he would know she was human.

"I don't know her," Chase spoke slowly, hoping it was the

last time he'd have to explain. "I've never met her before this morning. She didn't even give me her name." There, that should settle things. He didn't understand how she could feel so threatened over such an innocent encounter. He spotted his reserved parking spot and pulled into it.

"Oh that's just fine, Percy." Georgia quietly unclipped her seat belt and carefully opened the car door. "I'm sure it's nothing." She stepped out of the vehicle and shut the door with a controlled click. "If you don't want to talk about it I understand. Really." She gave him a tight smile and strode off toward the track entrance reserved for owners and V.I.P.'s.

"Georgia, I'm sorry." Though he didn't know what about. "I didn't mean to make you mad."

"I. Am. Not. Mad." She stopped long enough to make her declaration, then smiled sweetly at William, the gate guard, and continued through.

The guard shrugged at Chase and shot him a "my-wife-tells-me-the-same-thing" look. If this was what life with Georgia would hold for him, he wanted out now.

By the time he caught up to her she was climbing the stairs to his family's viewing box. For such a petite woman she could move with amazing speed. He decided to take a cue from her and pretend nothing was wrong. She would bring it up again when she was ready to talk—which would probably be on the ride home. He sighed audibly.

"Is something wrong, Junior?" his mother asked as she stood to peck her son on the cheek.

"Just a bit of a headache." He glanced at Georgia, but she was busy socializing with the Burkes, who held the box beside theirs. It seemed she liked nothing better than to show off with those in their social circle. He wondered if he really had anything in common with his Texan girlfriend.

"Your father's at the stables with the trainer," his mother broke into his thoughts. "He's very excited about this new horse of his."

After thirty-five years of marriage there was very little

Percival Dymond the Third got excited about. Fine thoroughbred horseflesh was his greatest vice. He established his own
stable before he got married and poured generous sums of
money into the training of his horses.

"I think I'll go down and check out his latest investment."
Chase was really interested in seeing his father's horse . . .
really.

Abby eyed the bucket of poultice she was about to plunge
her hands into. It wasn't her favorite job to do, but Chi-Chi's
tendons were swelling and she couldn't risk further injury
before the mare's next race. The gray clay squished between
her fingers and packed into her nails when she reached into
the bucket.

*My ex-mother-in-law spent hundreds of dollars at luxury
spas to play in the mud like this*, she thought, but the reas-
surance didn't help. Mud was mud, no matter what form it
came in.

One of her grooms held Chi-Chi's head and another
picked up her front left foot as Abby bent to her task. The
mare was bad tempered enough to try to kick even though
she was only standing on three legs. When she failed to hit
her target she snapped her teeth at her handler and nearly
took off his nose.

"Watch it, Jim," Abby warned.

"Don't worry about him, boss," Melanie spoke up.
"Maybe Chi-Chi can bite the bump off his nose and save
him the cost of plastic surgery."

"Want me to show you how I got this crooked nose, brat?"
Jim growled.

"I heard you got drunk, fell over and broke it on a bar
stool as you came down," Abby teased.

"Really?" Melanie asked. "I heard he got drunk, fell into
bed and hit the headboard on the way down."

"I was not drunk!" Jim whispered fiercely. He probably
would have roared it, but raising his voice would have in-

cited Chi-Chi to take another nip at him. "I was defending my honor."

"Over a woman," they stated in unison.

"Hmmph," Jim grunted. "I must have told you the story before."

"At least a hundred times," Abby said.

"More like a thousand," Melanie added.

Chi-Chi's leg was now thickly covered in poultice from hock to ankle. So were Abby's hands. This was quickly becoming a problem since her nose was beginning to itch, and if she didn't scratch it soon she was going to sneeze.

She glanced at her clay-smeared hands and her relatively clean jeans. She could try wiping the mud off on her pants but the stuff stuck to her skin like bubble gum to hair. She tried rubbing her face against her shoulder, but only made the itching sensation worse. It didn't help that she had horse-hair all over her T-shirt and now it was clinging to her face.

"Oh heck," she muttered.

"Problem, boss?" Jim asked.

"You might say so."

"Should I go get the track vet?"

"The vet?" It finally occurred to Abby; her stable hands weren't aware of her predicament. She grinned. How would she explain this to old Doc Casey? The man had no sense of humor. "I don't think he's necessary."

Giving up the fight, she let go of Chi-Chi's leg. She scratched her nose with both hands, closing her eyes and immersing herself in the pleasure. She could wipe her face off later. "Ahhh." She rocked back on her heels and exhaled. "Much better."

She opened her eyes to see both her stable grooms smirking at her.

"Every time," Jim stated.

"Like clockwork," Melanie seconded. "I think there's a nerve in your fingertips attached to your nose, boss. Whenever you have some sort of gunk on your hands your face starts to itch."

Abby shrugged and got back to work on the horse's leg. She wound paper over the poultice then reached for a stable bandage. In minutes the mare's leg was wrapped.

"Hey you might be onto something here, boss." Melanie's eyes sparkled as she put down Chi-Chi's leg and gingerly stepped away from the mare. "Jim could smear some of that stuff on his nose and try to shrink the lump."

"Imp," Jim growled. "I'm going to stick your face in the bucket of poultice and see if it relieves the swelling in your pretty little head. Something has to deflate your ego."

Melanie laughed and shook her blond mane at him like a mischievous mare. "You have to catch me first, old man."

"You have to sleep sometime, brat," Jim warned. An evil smile curled his lips.

Abby ignored the growling and threats. Jim would never hurt the young woman he secretly admired. She stood up and grabbed a towel from the nearby wash rack, attempting to wipe some of the mess off her hands. "I want Chi-Chi on a protein-reduced diet the next few days and in the morning, use a handful of Buchu leaves to reduce the swelling. No exercise, but walk her for thirty minutes everyday." Abby tossed the towel onto the wash pile.

"Got it, boss." Jim turned the mare around and took her down the row to her stall.

"Sweet mother," Melanie exhaled. "Look at that prime piece of stud muffin in a pair of sunglasses."

Abby was putting away her supplies and assessing her medicine chest so she didn't bother to look at Melanie's man. Her stable hand was always ogling someone when she wasn't being ogled herself. Her wavy blond hair and her big brown eyes could melt the heart of a snowman.

"Oh!" Melanie squealed. "He's coming this way!"

The bucket of poultice slipped from Abby's grasp and she bent to retrieve it. She wanted to get away before Melanie started to flirt with her newest man.

"Miss Blue?"

Abby stood up and spun around so fast she nearly fell

over. It wasn't one of Melanie's stud muffins standing in front of her—it was Chase Dymond. She opened her mouth to speak, but even a simple "hello" stuck. How could she have ever thought this man was cute? Towering over her with a frown creasing his brow he looked imposing, grim and gorgeous, but not remotely cute. The term described cuddly teddy-bear types, not Chase.

"What the—" his frown deepened. "What's on your face?"

Abby raised a hand to cover the poultice. She'd forgotten about it, but now that it was brought to her attention the drying mud began to itch like mad. She rubbed her nose and some of the clay crumbled off.

Chase looked around, then walked over to the wash rack, grabbed a rag, wetted it down and squeezed out the excess water before returning. "Here, use this," he said, handing it to her.

"Thanks." Abby's cheeks heated into a blush. She scrubbed at the poultice as best as she could without a mirror. When she finished she noticed Chase was still scrutinizing her face, or at least she supposed he was beneath his sunglasses.

"Let me." He took the rag from Abby and wrapped one of his large hands behind her neck. She found herself leaning into his warm grasp. He didn't smell like alcohol anymore. The light aftershave he wore made her want to burrow her nose in his neck and inhale.

Her eyes drifted closed as he raised the cloth to her face. She was lost in the spell of intimacy. Chase gently wiped away the rest of the poultice. She felt his knuckles brush her cheek so lightly they seemed like a soft summer breeze wafting past.

Abby opened her eyes and stared into the unchanging lenses of his sunglasses. She imagined he was looking straight into her heart and she shivered with the thought of what he might find there. The insecurities, fears and hurt left by her ex-husband still rested close to the surface. All those things left scars that marked her heart and aged her tired soul.

"Hey, boss!" Melanie waved her hand between them. "Are you going to introduce me to your friend?"

"My . . ." Abby looked from Mel to Chase. "He's not my friend. I mean, I don't really know him."

Melanie snorted. "Not what it looks like to me, boss."

Abby stepped out of Chase's hold. She wouldn't be able to get command of the situation again if she couldn't control herself and her furious blushing. "Mr. Dymond—"

"I thought I told you to call me Chase."

She brushed back a strand of hair that had escaped from her ponytail. "All right, Chase, this is—"

"Melanie, but most people call me, Mel. I am *so* pleased to meet you. I was beginning to think the boss was frigid, if you know what I mean. I've been working for her for over a year now and have never once seen her with a man."

"Hey!" Abby sputtered. *So much for gaining control of the situation.*

"There's no reason to be embarrassed, boss." Melanie turned to Chase. "She's just choosy. You should be flattered."

"Really?" He smiled.

"Do you have any idea who this is?" Abby asked Mel.

"Chase Dymond," Melanie responded with a wink to the man in question.

"Yeah, as in, Percival Chase Dymond the . . . whatever-number-you-are." She glanced at the grinning man then returned her attention to the scolding she was giving. "As in soon to be engaged, face scattered throughout the local newspapers and heir to his parents' fortune." She put her hands on her hips and glared down at her stable groom.

"Cool!" Melanie responded. "Way to go, boss. Are you his mistress, or something?" She covered her mouth with her hand then removed it. "Whoopsie, I shouldn't say that so loud. You never know who's listening."

"I give up." Abby groaned. "Don't you have some stalls to muck?"

"Sure, boss." Mel walked away, but stopped and shot her employer a devious grin, "You two need to steal all the private moments you can, right?"

"Jim's right, I should fire you," Abby called at Mel's retreating back. Her only response was a hardy laugh.

She became aware of Chase's quiet chuckle beside her. It affected her the same way the man did. Tingles stole up her spine and heat spread through her body. She had to stop the intimacy they shared before it went any further. "You'd do well to remember your place too, Mr. Dymond," she turned on him.

"And what place would that be?" he asked soberly.

"By your family's side." She paused, then added, "close to the purse strings."

"Maybe." The comment didn't seem to offend him, or keep him from brushing a pesky strand of hair off her face and back behind her ear. Both of her meetings with him had been the same. He was forward and flirty with her and not the least bit remorseful over his suggestiveness.

"Are you still drunk?" She blurted before she could stop the thought.

"No." He smiled at her. "And never again. It was really stupid, even if it was worth it."

"What do you mean?" She wondered what could possibly be good about getting drunk, then dealing with the hangover later.

"I never would have met you if my cabbie hadn't dropped me off at the wrong farm."

Abby frowned.

"*And* I would have had to wake up to an empty room, instead of your sweet face."

"This isn't right." She walked into her makeshift tack room. It was really a stall converted over for the purpose. She began mixing feed and vitamins for Melanie to give out in the evening. "You shouldn't be talking to me like this. You already have someone in your life, for goodness sakes."

"What isn't right is meeting you after her."

Abby couldn't look at him and she didn't dare articulate anything. As much as she agreed with Chase, it would be wrong to say so. He wasn't free for her to pursue a relationship with and even if he were, it would never work. She didn't belong in his world. She had learned it the hard way from her ex-husband, Martin, and his family.

"Abby?" he asked. "Did you hear me?"

She took a deep breath and shook off the unwelcome memories of her brief marriage. "I heard you, Mr. Dymond, and I think we should keep our relationship on a strictly business level. Since I can't see what business you'd have here, maybe you should leave." She turned to look at him.

"If that's the way you want it, I do have something I wish to discuss."

Oh great, she thought. *Now I've made him mad and he's going to sue me for hitting him this morning. When will I ever learn to keep my mouth shut and play nice?*

"What do you want from me?" She knew it was the wrong way to phrase her question when the corner of his mouth lifted into a smile. He was *not* thinking about money.

"I have a horse I want you to train."

"A horse?" She'd been watching the way his lips moved when he spoke and lost track of what they were talking about. With an effort, she formed her next question: "Why do you want me to train your horse? Your father has his own trainers."

"I'm not as tied to the family purse strings as you seem to think. I like doing things my own way. Will you take the job?"

"I don't think it's such a good idea." She shifted uncomfortably. "I could refer you to someone else if you'd like."

"I didn't want to get tough, Abby." Chase lowered his sunglasses. "But do I have to remind you, you owe me?"

The black circle around his eye was more accusing than the look he gave her. "You're blackmailing me?"

"If that's what it takes to get you to accept my offer . . . yes, I guess I am."

Suzanne Walter

"But why?"

Chase raised his glasses back over his eyes. "It's not very often I desire something enough to ask for it, but when I do I always get what I'm after."

Abby nodded, fuming silently. Now was not the time to lose her temper. She would talk to Julia and find a way out of this mess.

"I'll bring the horse to your farm tomorrow."

She watched him leave and wondered what Chase really wanted—because if he decided he wanted her, her troubles were just beginning.

Chapter Three

I have a horse I want you to train? Chase questioned his sanity as he walked toward his father's barn. "Where am I going to find a horse?"

A passing stable hand must have heard his comment, because he called back, "I don't know, buddy. Maybe you should try the zoo."

Chase decided it would be best to keep his thoughts to himself. The thing was, when it came to Abby he seemed to lose his head and do things he wouldn't normally do—like talking to himself, and telling her she would be working with a horse that, at the moment, didn't exist. When she had said she would only deal with him in a business relationship he had congratulated himself for thinking so fast and telling her about the horse. He hadn't considered the fact he didn't actually have one.

In truth, Chase was unsettled by his interest in Abby. He should not be considering her at all. He was technically involved with Georgia and even if he weren't in love with her she was his parents' ideal of what his girlfriend should be. He had stopped looking for a perfect love a long time ago. It was unfair Fate should tempt him with the kind of woman who could fulfill his old dream now. He needed to prove to himself he only wanted Abby because he couldn't have her. Once he spent some time around her he was sure the impulses he was experiencing would wear off.

He hoped.

Until then, he had to talk his father into letting him use one of his horses. Percy Sr. would be thrilled his son was taking an interest in the sport he valued more than his business. He would be appalled to find out Chase was only doing it to secure some time with a woman. If Percy hadn't irresponsibly poured his money into his thoroughbreds his son might not be in this position now anyway.

Throughout Chase's life his parents drilled his family obligations into him. It was his responsibility to up hold their name, to act respectable in public and to one day take over the business. After he graduated from college he rebelled against them. He moved to New York and pursued a career of his own until the fateful day he got his mother's phone call.

His father's fortune was dwindling due to the money he was pouring into his thoroughbreds and the Dymond Enterprises Advertising Firm was steadily losing income because of an incompetent president. According to his mother, it was all Chase's fault, since he didn't assume his family duty and take over the business. It was time for him to come home.

He had already been dating Georgia when he got the news, and naturally he told her about the situation. She offered to go back home with him to provide support and possibly drum up some business for Dymond Enterprises in the form of her father's company. Chase had been planning to bring her with him when he went home for his best friend Al's wedding, so it seemed to make sense for her to spend the whole summer in Balesworth. He hadn't expected her to talk to his parents about their supposedly upcoming engagement—an engagement she hadn't even talked to him about.

The Dymond Dust barn came into view. "Junior," his father bellowed. "Come meet my new trainer."

The man his father talked about was short, slim and dark. He looked like one of the wild dogs that sometimes roamed the fields near the local farms. They were only dangerous when they were hungry. This was another member of the pack pulling down his father's fortune.

"Michael Dover, this is my son. Shake his hand, Junior."

Chase smiled and made nice for his father's sake. "I hope I'm not interrupting anything."

"Of course not. Michael was just telling me about the jockey he's hired to run this race."

"Really?" Chase focused his attention on the man. "And who would he be?"

"Alphonse Currero."

The jockey's name triggered Chase's memory. He was known for his aggressive riding style and heavy whipping— whether the horse needed it or not. "Interesting choice. I suppose Dad's horse is a little on the lazy side, requires more incentive to run."

"Lazy!" his father bellowed. "Hell, no! She's a rocket, ain't she, Mike? All fire that one. The pony riders can barely hold her back when she goes out for her morning warm-up."

"Seems a little unnecessary to put such an aggressive jockey on her if she's so anxious to run. She could get out of control, don't you think?" Chase looked pointedly at Michael.

"Alphonse gets results. Good enough for me."

He shrugged and let it go. Michael was his father's problem, not his.

"So Junior, what brings you out to the backstretch and away from your pretty lady's side?"

"I want to buy a horse from you."

"Buy it? Son, I'll give you a horse if you want one; but why the sudden interest?"

Chase searched for an answer that would best satisfy his father. "It looks like I'm going to be a permanent resident of Balesworth and I need a hobby to keep me busy."

"You're going to be learning how to run my company. Should be enough to keep you occupied, don't you think?"

Percy wasn't fooling his son. The company only kept his hands and his mind busy. His heart was completely involved in racing his horses. "I'm sure I can find the time to do something else. After all a man needs a hobby."

His father broke out into a wide grin. "That's my boy! I knew horses had to be in your blood. We'll go out to the barns when we get home and you can pick one out, then I'll have Michael start working with her right away."

"Whoa! Hold on. I already have a trainer."

"Oh . . . really?" The thought seemed to slow Percy down. "Who? Because I've got to tell you Michael is the best there is."

This month, Chase thought grimly. By the end of the season his father would be looking for his next "best trainer." Michael would be yesterday's news. "I've hired Abigail Blue, from Shady Blue Stables."

"You did what?!" Percy's face turned a deep shade of crimson.

Michael smirked, but he didn't leave. Apparently, he had no intention of missing the developing scene.

It wasn't the reaction Chase had expected. He really didn't think his father was so attached to his current trainer. It had never happened before. "I hired Abby. She's the woman who dropped me off at the house this morning."

"I thought she looked familiar! Trying to hide her long, dark mane under a ball cap was pretty clever. The little fox. How dare she step foot on my land!"

"Dad, calm down. We're not exactly the Hatfields and McCoys. What did she do to make you so mad?"

"She beat Mariah's Gold."

"Abby hit your horse?" Chase was being deliberately obtuse. He couldn't see what the big deal was. This was thoroughbred racing, and there was always a better horse.

"No, son. Her horse won Mariah's race. My mare was going to be a champion and that good-for-nothing woman and her mangy, flea-bitten excuse for a horse stole the race. It's a crime, I tell you. A crime! She probably cheated."

Realization hit Chase like a runaway horse. "You tried to hire her as a trainer, didn't you?" He suppressed a smile. "*And* she turned you down." People didn't say "no" to Percy Dymond. Abby had to have a backbone of steel to stand up to his father and win.

"I did no such thing!" Percy bellowed.

Sure his suspicion was right, Chase pursued the argument. "You offered her an obscene amount of money and she still refused to work with you."

"The woman is a nut! She said she had other clientele to consider and a stable the size of mine would take up all her time and resources."

Chase laughed. He couldn't help it. Abby refused to be bought and Percy didn't understand why. His father had never met a person he couldn't buy.

"This isn't funny, son. You're consorting with the enemy. I insist you fire her at once."

"I just hired her and I have no reason to let her go. Besides, I owe her." He owed it to Abby to show her he wasn't such a bad guy, and if he had to blackmail her to get her to see it, he would.

"I forgot she brought you home after you'd been missing all night. Tell me you didn't get tangled up in those arms of hers and now she's using your indiscretion to control you."

"*Sweet,*" Michael murmured, then coughed to cover his slip.

"I already told you I passed out in her barn after being dropped off at the wrong place. Abby found me and brought me home. Nothing happened."

"Doesn't matter. She's dangerous to you, son. If you won't consider your girlfriend, I will. Stay away from Abigail Blue, or I won't give you a horse."

Chase knew Percy didn't care about Georgia, but he was awfully fond of her parents' fortune. He had hoped his father wouldn't be so difficult—he should have known better. "I guess I'll have to buy a horse from someone else."

"Good luck," Michael snorted. "It's the beginning of the

racing season. No one's looking to sell right now. They might have a winner."

"Oh, *please*! There's not a person out there who won't sell if the price is right."

"Your Ms. Blue wouldn't agree," Percy reminded him.

"No, but you were trying to buy her, not her horse."

Chase turned to leave with his father trailing after him. He was back in the grandstand before Percy stopped ranting at him.

"What's wrong with your father?" Sara Dymond asked. "He's turning purple."

"Maybe you should ask your son what's wrong. Forget it, I'll tell you. Junior has lost his mind!"

"Really, Percy! Show a little class, people are staring at us."

"That's because they can't believe the heir to the Dymond empire has no sense. They're probably wondering whose side of the family it came from." He glared at the growing number of spectators. "It wasn't mine!"

Chase sunk down in his seat. Percy and his famous temper were making a spectacle of the family again. He glanced at Georgia and shivered from the cold stare she gave him.

"Well, he certainly doesn't get it from me," Sara said. "But his breeding is not the point, is it? What did he do to make you so mad?"

"He hired a crazy woman to train his horse for him."

"She's not crazy, Dad."

"Darling," Georgia put a hand on his thigh, "you're speaking out of turn. Let your father finish."

"Like I said, he hired that crazy Abigail Blue to train his horse."

"Who's she?"

"She's the same woman who dropped Junior off at the house this morning."

"Really?" Georgia's smile was as friendly as a rattlesnake's. "I thought you didn't know her—hadn't met her before this morning."

Her hand tightened on Chase's thigh and he could feel the prick of her nails through his pants. What he wouldn't give for a crowbar and a nail file right now. He ignored her and continued on, "She's a good trainer. Her horse beat Mariah's Gold."

"That mare?" His mother laughed. "A monkey riding an egg beater could out run her."

"Sara! I will not have my wife talking trash about me or my horses."

"Oh put a sock in it, Percy, and stop being so melodramatic. I'm on your side." She looked at Chase. "Do you really think it's wise to hire a woman you know nothing about to train a horse for you?"

"I think I owe her as much. She did take me home after she found me in her barn. She could have told me to walk, or called the police."

"Then send her flowers, dear. You don't owe her anything more. A bouquet of roses costs more than a cab ride from her farm to ours."

She's worth more than a handful of dying flowers, but he didn't dare voice his opinion. "I've already hired her, so there's no point in discussing this any further."

Chase's mom glanced at Georgia and shook her head before returning her attention to him. "You're as bullheaded as your father. Do you even think before you act?"

"I—never mind."

Georgia added her opinion to the argument, "I think it's great that you're getting involved in racing, but is a female trainer best?" She was all smiles and affection, but an unmistakable glint of jealousy burned in her eyes. "Of course, *I* would never dream of telling you what to do."

"I'm glad you understand," Chase said, choosing to ignore her meaning. "If you don't mind going home with my parents, I have to go find a horse."

"You don't have a horse?" Her voice rose slightly and her tightly held composure slipped a notch. "You hired that woman first?"

"Yes, I did." He raised an eyebrow. "This isn't a problem, is it?"

"Uh . . . no," She balled her hands into fists. "Why wouldn't you hire a trainer first? She's as necessary as the horse."

"That's what I thought. I'm so glad we see eye to eye about this." He slipped out of his seat and kissed her on the cheek before leaving. "I'll see you tonight at dinner." Then he jogged down the stairs before his parents could call him back and lecture him some more about the wisdom of hiring Abigail Blue as his trainer.

"You can't be serious!" Julia curled her petite form into the couch. "You almost killed him and he asked you to train his horse?"

Abby shrugged her shoulders. She didn't understand it either.

"You must have hit him harder than you thought." She ran her hand through her short, spiky, brown hair and grinned. "Think what he would have asked for if you had really beaned him."

Chase had already asked for a kiss, what else did he want from her? She shifted uncomfortably in her chair. "If I'd hit him any harder he'd have been in a coma." And then she would *really* owe him.

How far did he intend to take his extortion? She really didn't know him well enough to say. And how far would she go to save her stable and her friends' livelihoods? A shiver ran through her as she imagined Chase's rich voice asking her to kiss him. A rush of excitement flooded her. Would she actually be able to refuse him if he asked? And if she did kiss him, would it be a noble sacrifice to save her friends, or a selfish act to fulfill her own desires?

"Earth to Abby!" Julia snapped her fingers a few times. "Are you still with me?"

"Yeah." She ran her hands down her thighs and thought about icebergs. "You lost me for a moment."

"I noticed. Where were you?"

"I was off riding horses across deserted beaches. Where else would I be?"

"I'm not sure daydreaming about riding horses has ever given you such a rosy flush." Julia got off the couch and moved toward the kitchen. She returned with a glass of lemonade in each hand and passed one to Abby as she returned to the sofa. "So, is he cute?"

"Is who cute?"

"Unless I'm wrong, which I'm not, Chase Dymond. You know, the guy you've been riding off into the sunset with."

"Gorgeous." Abby slapped a hand over her mouth. "Why do you ask?" she mumbled between her fingers.

"When will you ever learn not to question the all knowing mind of Jules the Great?"

Abby removed her hand from her lips. "She sees all. She knows all. Scary thought!"

"Rob thinks so."

"I got a call from my brother last night. Marni's pregnant."

"Better her than me. How far along is she?"

"Three months." Jake had been a confirmed bachelor until he met Marni. Abby didn't think she had ever known him to be happier.

"So she's due in October?"

Abby nodded.

"I'm really happy for them. Now, quit changing the subject and tell me how Mr. Chase Dymond convinced you to train a horse for him. You turned his father down flat when he made the same request."

Since her diversion tactics weren't working, she decided to sate her friend's curiosity. "I know I did, but Chase only has one horse, not a stable full of them. He also doesn't have his father's reputation for dropping his trainer for a new one each year. If we gave up all our other clients for Percy and he fired us we'd lose everything. As for convincing me, please recall how I gave him a black eye this morning. How much is ownership of this stable worth to you?"

Julia sat up on the couch. Loud indignation replaced the teasing tone in her voice. "Wait just one lousy minute! He was the one who was trespassing, yet he's *forcing* you to train his horse?"

"Blackmail? Yes, though he didn't say it in so many words. I think an assault charge would carry more strength behind it than one for trespassing."

"That-that scum!" Julia sputtered. "He's as worthless as a large, steaming pile of horse-apples. No, scratch that, even horse-apples are good for fertilizer. He's good for nothing. What are we going to do about him? I'm up for revenge."

"We can't."

Julia huffed and threw herself into the back of the couch, crossing her arms and wiggling her foot furiously. "Why not?"

"Because as fun as it would be, we're in no position to deal with a lawsuit and if we make him mad he might decide to go after the stable as payback. Our liability insurance covers horse-human accidents, but I don't think they'll back us in a human-human incident, even if it did happen in the barn." Abby sighed. "It really could be worse, at least he's paying us."

"Well the money is something, but it's still not right." Julia stopped bouncing her foot, a sure sign her temper was cooling. "We went together in this business so we could choose our own clients and have some control over the horses we deal with. We moved from Texas to start a new life, not relive the old one."

"We moved to escape my past," Abby muttered, suddenly depressed by the turn of the conversation.

"Stop that right now."

"Stop what?"

"The long face and the moping. You are not allowed to feel guilty over what your ex-husband and his rotten family did to you."

"If it wasn't for the lies and the scandal they created for

me I wouldn't have had to drag you all the way from Texas to Kentucky."

"You didn't drag me anywhere, I volunteered. They scarred my reputation too. We were both lucky to get out of Tumbleweed Downs with a few cents to our names and the clothes on our backs."

"The point is, Martin and his family went after you because of me. I couldn't be the perfect, socialite daughter-in-law."

"More like you wouldn't bow down to their stupid rules and you hated being a snob. And please don't forget that your ex was a womanizing playboy."

"You thought I was a snob?"

"Well . . . maybe." Julia gave her a teasing grin. "Okay, not really, but your in-laws sure were. Martin's mother could freeze the toes off a penguin with the icy stare she used to give everyone."

Abby laughed. "I know, did I ever tell you how much they saved on central air?"

"You were too good for his family."

"I was too blind to see what Martin's parents were up to and too weak to fight for him."

"Abby, I have never known you to be weak. The only reason you're not with Martin is because *you* chose to walk away. I, for one, am glad you did and doubly glad I came with you. I wouldn't have found Rob if I hadn't ended up in Kentucky with you."

"You're right. Both our lives got better when we moved here, but sometimes I can't shake the feeling my marriage failed because I wasn't strong enough to make it work."

Julia snorted. "I know how to make you feel better."

"How?"

"Girls night out at Margaritaville!" She launched herself off the couch and over to the phone. "I'll call Mel and have her get the word out to the gang. It'll be a blast."

"Julia, I don't really feel like dancing."

"Sure you do. We have a new client! Let's celebrate tonight, then tomorrow we'll figure out how to make Chase Dymond pay for blackmailing you."

Four hours and several stables later, Chase stood beside Theodore Jamison at a pasture gate somewhere on Theo's massive estate. Chase suspected his father had called in some favors because no one had a horse they wanted to sell him.

Theo cracked open the gate and waited for Chase to slip through before he followed and shut it again. The spring had brought heavy rains this year and the ground was muddy around the entrance. Chase looked at his feet and sighed. He'd have to start carrying a spare set of clothes in his car. The day's events were enough to convince him.

"Have I told you what his bloodlines are?"

"Uh . . . no." He looked around the overgrown pasture, but didn't see any horses. Had Theo been hitting the bottle early today?

"He's part Yorkshire Terrier, part Greyhound and partly from a good neighborhood!" The portly man laughed robustly at his own joke. "Just kidding." He slapped Chase on the back. "He's Lancelot on top and Mighty Dot on the bottom."

"Oh." Chase had never heard of either line, but it really didn't matter. He was desperate for a horse and this man had one he was willing to sell. "Um, Theo, have you noticed there's no horses in this field."

"Huh?" He glanced around. "Sure there is. He's probably just in the lean-to. We keep him isolated from the others because he's a stud colt. Don't want him breeding before his time." He gave a wink, then turned and whistled loudly into the pasture.

Chase hadn't bargained on the colt being a stallion, it could drive up the price. He heard the sound of hooves running through the grass and noticed a horse coming up over a slight rise in the field. The animal let out a deep whinny as he ran toward them. He slid to a stop at the edge of the mucky entrance and splattered mud on Chase's suit jacket before walking sedately up to the gate.

The rangy colt wasn't a bay, nor was he a chestnut; he was more or less the color of the mud he stood in. His coat, which should have been shiny and trim by this time of year, was shaggy and dull.

Theodore grabbed the colt's halter and attempted to stand him up square so Chase could have a look at his legs. He was cow-hocked in the back and turned out on the front. The four legs, that should have been an asset to a horse, stuck out at all corners. Chase shook his head. *Leave it to Jamison to own a horse who looks like he's been on a twelve-day drinking binge.*

"Well, what do you think?" Theodore's red nose glowed with pride. "His name is Lancelot's Mighty Sword."

"I don't know, Theo. He's not exactly what I'm looking for." Not that he had much choice at this point. He'd wasted the day talking to people his father had gotten to first, and now it was starting to get dark and he was faced with only two choices: Buy this horse, or admit to Abby he didn't have one for her to train.

He risked stepping closer to the colt and hoped he wasn't as mean as he was ugly. The horse looked at Chase cautiously, then reached out tentative lips to pluck at his jacket sleeve. Deciding he was safe, he pulled from Theo's grip and surprised Chase by plunging his head into his chest and wuffling heartily as a sign of greeting and approval.

"Oh, Lance *really* likes you."

Chase smiled, starting to like the horse despite his flaws. He knelt down to take a closer look at his legs and found they were clean of splints and nicks—a miracle considering Lance didn't have very straight legs. Standing back up, Chase noticed the colt had a short back and muscular hindquarter. He could have some speed and he might not be such a bad buy after all. "Did you have a price in mind?" he asked casually.

He almost swore he could see dollar signs dancing in Theodore's eyes. The portly man licked his lips greedily, eyeing the horse like his last meal.

"I couldn't take less than ten thousand dollars for this fine animal."

It would be rude to laugh. "Out of the question."

"But his fine breeding!"

"I've never heard of either of his parents."

"What about his regal carriage?"

"Theo, this horse has a shaggy coat, mud covering most of his body and is in desperate need of a trim from a blacksmith. Do you honestly think he looks regal?"

"I suppose I could lower my price to eight thousand, but you're robbing me, old friend."

Robbing him? The two-hundred-acre estate was only one of five houses the Jamisons owned around the world. The thing robbing Theo was his health due to his excessive drinking. "The horse needs to see a vet and he probably has worms. I'll give you five thousand and even at that he's grossly over-priced."

"You *wound* me sir!" Theodore feigned a direct hit to his heart, which had apparently migrated to the right side of his chest. When he saw his theatrics had failed to impress anyone, including the horse he was defending, he conceded.

Chase shook his head. His instincts told him the other man would cave if he were pushed. "Sorry Theo, I was under the impression you wanted to sell this horse. I suppose I'll have to consider other options." It was a lie—he had no options, but what Theo didn't know wouldn't hurt him.

Gently pushing the colt away from the gate, Chase exited the pasture and walked toward his parked car. He heard hurried steps and puffing behind him.

"Wait!"

He stopped and looked at his shoes, pretending he had no other care in the world than the mud on them. He waited for the other man to catch up before he turned to look at him.

"Five-thousand, five-hundred, and I get first option to buy Lance back if you decide to sell him."

Theo had a right to his pride, and the extra five-hundred dollars was nothing to haggle over. Chase reached out his hand and took Theo's in a firm shake. "Deal. I'll drop off the check and pick up the horse in the morning."

As Chase got in his car and followed the dirt path out to the road, he thought about Abby. He could picture her long brown hair, sparkling eyes and generous smile. *I hope she doesn't laugh too hard when she gets a look at Lance and I tell her he's a racehorse.*

Chapter Four

"**I**s this a joke?" Abby stood in her barn and looked at the scruffy horse Chase had brought her to train—at least the colt had a leg at each corner, too bad that was his best feature. Long, mud-caked hair covered his body, except for a few patches where he had rubbed it off, hair and all. The worst part was, he was all hers and Chase didn't look like he was kidding.

"What's wrong with him?"

Chase wore sunglasses, a light-blue, button-up shirt with the sleeves rolled up and navy dress pants. He looked like he should be on the cover of a magazine, not standing in a barn with one very unkempt horse.

"What isn't wrong with him?" Abby sized up the horse again. "Has he *ever* seen a brush?"

"You didn't give me much time to find—" Chase stopped abruptly.

"Find what?" Abby glared at him. "A horse? Have you been putting me on? Did you just buy a horse so you'd have a reason to hang around me?" She crossed her arms and gave him her best glower. Maybe she could still get rid of Chase and keep her life from getting too complicated.

"No! A brush . . . I needed a brush to clean him up, but I didn't have enough time to do that so I brought him like he was."

Abby knew he was lying, but she couldn't prove it. "This horse needs more than a brush. He needs a veterinarian, a good worming and a blacksmith. Never mind the fact I'm going to have to keep him in quarantine until I can hose him down and see if there's actually a horse underneath all the mud."

She stifled the urge to shake her head and sigh. The poor thing looked awful. "I can't believe you want me to train this animal for you. Is this the only one your father would let you take off the farm when he found out I'd be training it?"

"No." A brief frown crossed Chase's strong features. "Lance is the horse I want you to train."

"Lance?"

"Yeah. His name is Lancelot's Mighty Sword."

A giggle escaped Abby. It was such a silly name for such a sad-looking horse. She wasn't sure Lance would ever be a *mighty* anything, but she'd give him her best shot. She had a reputation to maintain as a trainer.

"All right, Mr. Dymond. I'll see what I can do with Lance. I'll get the vet and the farrier out to see him as soon as possible. Why don't you come back in a week to check on his progress?" Abby didn't wait for his answer; instead, she walked into the tack room to get an economy-sized bottle of shampoo, a bucket and an extra-large sponge.

"I'm afraid that won't be possible."

Chase was standing so close behind her she dropped her sponge in surprise. "Th—that's okay. You can come back in two weeks if it's more convenient."

She bent to retrieve the lost item, but Chase was still behind her and bending with her. His large hand enclosed around her fingers and the sponge. He was so close she could barely breathe. He smelled like soap and she could detect the slightest hint of his delicious aftershave. If she leaned back, just a little bit, she'd be enveloped by his warmth.

"I'm afraid you don't understand, Abby. I like to take a hands-on approach to having my horse trained. I want to be there every step of the way so I can see what you're doing."

He pulled her up with him as he straightened.

She was glad he was holding onto her because her knees were as weak as a newborn foal's. "I—I could take notes," she stammered.

"I'm more of a visual person." He released her hand and it dropped with the sponge into the bucket.

"Is anybody in—is that a horse?"

Abby jumped away from Chase and bumped into the shelf in her hurry to get away from him. He was standing too close. She wrapped her arms tightly around the bucket and moved past him into the barn aisle. As long as he wasn't touching her, she could keep her senses.

"I'm right here, Julia. Yes, that's a horse . . . I think. We'll find out as soon as I wash some of the mud off him."

Abby eyed the horse and then her best friend. "How about you get started with him and I'll call the vet?" She thrust the bucket in Julia's direction.

"Oh no! I'm your partner, not your slave. Why don't you have Mr. Dymond do it? I assume this is his horse."

"Good point." Abby turned to Chase. "Care to give your horse a bath?"

"Wouldn't mind, but I'm not really dressed to help out."

"It would make things up to me for not brushing him before you brought him here," she coaxed.

"But I have to go to the office this afternoon."

"It's still early. You'll have time to change your clothes."
Chase hesitated.

"You said you wanted to take a hands-on approach to training your horse."

"All right . . . I'll do it." He took the bucket from her.

"Great!" Julia broke in, clearly relieved she wasn't stuck with the dirty job. "Abby, I'm going to catch up on some of the work in your office, so I can call the vet for you while I'm in there."

"Thanks. Tell him to bring wormer with him and call the farrier too, while you're at it."

Julia left and Abby snapped a lead-rope on Lance before unhooking him from the cross-ties. "Come on, studly. Let's get this over with."

"What did you just call me?"

"I called *your horse* studly. For you, I have some other names." She tied Lance to the outdoor wash-rack.

"Like what?"

She stepped back and held the hose out to Chase. "Like 'slave.' Get washing."

Abby had to admit he was being a very good sport about the whole thing. He didn't gripe or complain about being put to work. Instead, he put down the bucket, pushed his sleeves up and took the hose from her.

"I would probably soak him down with the hose first and then use the shampoo on him," she suggested. "Start with his legs so he can get used to the water temperature, then work your way up."

"You're the boss." Chase shrugged. He turned and sprayed Lance's legs.

As the first few drops of water hit the young horse, he danced in place and tried to avoid the impending soaking. After a few minutes of prancing and snorting, Lance started to relax. It wasn't long before he lowered his head and sedately gnawed on the wooden fence rail he was tied to. Abby thought the colt might be enjoying his bath. She knew if the situation were reversed she would be happy to get all the mud out of her hair.

She admired the way Chase's shoulders strained against his dress shirt. He had really great shoulders. Strong enough to carry a world of problems on them . . . "Stop that!" He turned around and she noticed his startled expression.

"Stop what? Am I doing something wrong?"

"Uh . . . no. It's not you. I mean . . . that is to say . . . I should stop standing around here and go up to the house to check on Julia. Will you be okay by yourself for a few minutes?"

"Yeah. Could you bring me a towel on your way back?" He looked down at his damp clothing. "I think I'm going to need it."

"Sure." Abby retreated before she did anything foolish—like offer him a warm embrace in exchange for the towel.

Chase watched Abby until the barn blocked her from his view. Then he imagined he could still see her great figure and the way her steady stride caused her long, dark ponytail to swing back and forth across her back.

He recalled the tingling sensation he had gotten in his palms when he touched her in the barn. He wanted to hold her again; see if he got the same reaction, or if he was just imagining it. He didn't understand how something as simple as a touch could be so satisfying and so unfulfilling all at the same time.

Lance snorted, drawing Chase's attention back to the task at hand. The colt looked more like a dripping, wet, mongrel dog than a thoroughbred racehorse. He certainly wasn't a "king" among his breed. "Time for the soap, buddy."

Chase poured a generous amount of the thick green liquid into the bucket and prayed it was extra strength. He added water until bubbles frothed up and spilt over the sides. He dipped in the sponge and when it was sufficiently loaded with suds he slapped it onto Lance's sopping coat. The horse grunted, but didn't fuss.

The bucket had to be filled a second time before Lance was fully soaped-up. Vigorously rubbing in a clockwise motion, Chase lost himself in his thoughts. Had it really only been one day since Abby had knocked him out in her barn? It seemed she had been the only thing he could think about since.

Chase groaned. He had to get a hold of himself and stop

thinking about her. She was just a woman. A woman he couldn't have, thanks to Georgia.

"I should be thinking about the Tiessen account I'm going to be working on." He was supposed to call Georgia's father from the office today to discuss advertising plans for his company. He was stumped. In New York he'd been the junior accounts manager for a large textile company. He knew how to crunch numbers, but not much else.

Lance ignored him and continued to gnaw on the fence rail he was tied to. Chase thought about some of the previous ad campaigns Tiessen's Tidy Toilet Accessories had used. At first, Mr. and Mrs. Tiessen acted as spokespeople for their products, then they tried some cartoon spots and the classic "Why You Should Buy Our Products" ads. Could he propose anything different?

Some of his favorite commercials used comedy to sell a product. The problem was, with the Tiessen account comedy would immediately equal toilet humor. It probably wasn't the best way to impress Georgia's family.

Then again, hanging around Abby to get a better look at her great legs wasn't very endearing either. *Hmmmm... Abby in bikini with only a tan covering her long, silky legs... sexy commercials are always popular—*

"Uggh!" Blobs of soap splattered all over the place as Lance shook out his coat like a dog. Chase took off his sunglasses and wiped the streaming mess from his face. He heard giggling behind him and swung around to find Abby about ten feet away, holding a fluffy pink towel. Enough was enough! He tossed his sunglasses on to the grass, grabbed the hose out of the bucket and twisted open the spout. A clean spray of water hit her full force smack in the middle of her chest.

"Chase!" she screamed, unsuccessfully trying to block the blast with her hands. She dropped the soaking wet towel at her feet and ran toward him.

She leapt at the hose, but he guessed what she was up to

and held it out of her reach. "Fair's fair, Abby. Why should I have all the fun—"

She had grabbed the sponge to use as a weapon and now he was spitting bubbles out of his mouth. He wiped his lips with the back of his hand. "This is war!"

Abby darted across the yard as quick as a cat. She still carried the sponge, so Chase grabbed the bucket of soapy water before he took off after her. She ran behind a large oak tree and peeked around the trunk at him.

"You wouldn't dare!" she squealed, staring at his bucket.

"Wouldn't I?" Chase grinned. He sloshed the bucket around for effect. "Of course, I could be persuaded to relinquish my weapon."

"What would it take? I'll get you another towel *and* I promise not to make you give Lance another bath . . . ever."

"Not good enough, Abby."

"One free week of training," she bargained.

"Nope."

"I'll cook you dinner."

"Uh . . . no."

"What do you want? There's not much more I can afford to give you."

"I want a kiss."

The statement hung in the air between them. Chase didn't know why he had asked for something so outrageous; he had Georgia and her kisses. But once the request was made he found he couldn't take it back.

After several anxious moments of waiting for her to say something, anything, he decided to give her an easy out. "I'll go finish bathing Lance. You can think about it." He turned and began to walk away.

Whap! Water and soapsuds rolled down the back of his neck.

"You forgot your sponge."

He spun around and glared at Abby. She was sticking her tongue out at him. He laughed despite himself.

"I'll go get some more towels," she said. "Leave Lance on the cross-ties and meet me in the house when you're done."

Chase had the horse rinsed and blanketed a quickly as he could manage. The colt's appearance now looked better than his own. Dirty and wet, Chase bore a striking resemblance to Lance's original appearance.

"Good thing looks aren't everything, buddy." If Abby was judging him by his, then he was already out of the game. He didn't believe it for a minute.

Chase jogged over to the house, but instead of swinging the door open and rushing in, he knocked. He didn't want to risk Abby throwing something at him again. The woman had deadly aim.

"Come on in."

The door opened and a towel was thrust at him.

"I changed my mind. Dry off a bit first, *then* come in."

He was disappointed to see she had changed her clothes already. He liked the wet T-shirt look on her. "You wouldn't have something warm and dry I could put on, would you?"

"Unless you want to wear my short, pink terry-cloth robe . . . no."

"I think I'll pass."

"Do you always treat your employees like this?" Abby frowned at him.

"Like what?"

"Oh . . . you know . . . dousing them with water, flirting madly with them and then trying to kiss them."

"I don't kiss Roger. He's a little old for me and not really my type."

"And I'm your type?" She put the question to him like an accusation.

"No, actually you're not." Chase sat on one of the barstools at her kitchen counter. "You're too tall."

"My hair's brown, not blond."

"Hmmm . . ." he nodded, agreeing with her.

"And it's too straight."

"Yeah . . . a lot of guys like curls."

"I'm too skinny, too mouthy and my legs are too long."

"You're legs are perfect."

"Really?"

"Yes."

"But you said I was too tall."

"Only for some men." He stood up to prove he wasn't one of those men.

"You said I wasn't your type."

"People's preferences change all the time, mine just did." He closed in on her.

"This has to stop." Abby put her hands on her hips and glared at him. "It's wrong. I'm supposed to be your employee and you have a girlfriend."

"You're right." He took a step back, giving her more than just physical space. "If you'll still train my horse then I promise I won't flirt anymore . . ." She took his offered hand and shook it. ". . . with Roger."

"Chase! You have to stop flirting with me, not Roger."

"Sorry Abby, but you already shook on it and a deal is a deal."

"You're not playing by the rules." She tried to pull her hand away, but he held firm.

"I'm tired of following the rules, they haven't gotten me anything I want." He pulled her closer to him so she had to look up into his face. "So, what do you say Abby, want to play with me?"

"No." She yanked her hand from his grasp. "I don't play games, especially not ones I don't understand. I *do* train horses and yours is going to take a considerable amount of work. In fact, I'm not sure I'll be able to give him the attention he needs in order to be a racehorse. Are you sure you still want me to train him?"

In a few short sentences she'd managed to turn the conversation away from his flirtation and back to business. She'd even found an opening to try to weasel out of their agreement, but Chase had worked too hard to let her go so easily. "I don't expect miracles from you and I realize you have other clients. I just want you to spend as much time with Lance as you would with anyone else's horse. We'll see how he comes along and take his training from there."

Abby stepped back and crossed her arms over her chest, regarding him silently. "That's all you want? Just to be treated like the other people I train horses for?"

"Actually I said I wanted you to treat my horse like anyone else's. I was hoping you would treat me differently."

"Differently?" One corner of her mouth lifted into a smile.

"Yeah, you know what I mean . . . special preference."

"Oh, you're definitely *special*."

He noticed her eyes positively sparkled with mischief. *She's up to something.*

"You already said you wanted to be part of the training. I think 'hands-on' was the way you put it?"

"Yeah . . ."

"We feed and do stalls at five in the morning. If you don't know how to use a pitchfork I'll show you."

"Abby, I didn't mean—"

"And since you wanted to be part of the training, you can help me break Lance to ride. I expect you know how to ride?"

"Yes . . . no . . . I haven't been on a horse since I was ten years old."

"Then you'll need lessons. I have an old mare I can put you on. You can have your lessons right after you finish the stalls each morning."

"Abby."

"Don't worry, I won't charge you extra. We'll consider your work in the barn payment in trade for your riding lessons."

"Abby!"

"What?" She smiled up at him innocently. "I thought you wanted special treatment."

She truly had a gift for making his life more difficult than he expected it would be. "Never mind. I'll be here at 5:00

a.m. and still be able to make it to the office before 10:00. I can work later to make up for the time I spend here."

"Good. You can start with going out to the barn before you leave, and putting Lance in the last stall on the left."

"I thought we'd be getting started today."

"Nope, we're not doing anything with Lance until I get the vet and the blacksmith out to see him." She walked to the door and opened it, gesturing for him to leave. "I'll see you first thing in the morning."

Chase walked to the door and leaned against the frame. "Aren't you forgetting something?"

"No . . . I don't think so."

"What about the kiss you still owe me?"

Abby moved so fast he was stumbling through the door before he realized she had pushed him. She swung the screen closed and he heard the lock click as she stood smiling smugly at him from the other side.

"You're going to have to be quicker than that if you want to corner me into a kiss." She waved goodbye, and he turned and walked slowly down the steps.

He realized the problem with Abby wasn't that she was proving herself so hard to get, it was that the challenge she presented was getting more and more intriguing to pursue.

"So how did things go with our new client?"

Abby turned from the kitchen window, where she had been watching Chase get into his car and admiring the way his damp shirt clung to his broad shoulders. He had a body like a work of art and a face just as pleasing. She couldn't believe he wanted her.

"Hmm . . ." she sighed, and with effort she returned her attention to Julia. "He's the most stubborn, persistent, arrogant, flirtatious man I've ever had to work with and I'm still attracted to him."

"Even I have to admit he's very good-looking."

Abby pinched the bridge of her nose. "What am I going to do?"

"You're not going to do anything. What you're both experiencing is just lust. It'll wear off, you'll train his horse and he'll continue to date Georgia."

"And if it doesn't wear off?"

"If it doesn't then you're not signing a prenuptial agreement this time." Julia winked at her and smiled wickedly. "We could use the extra money."

"With my luck his parents would disown him and I'd be stuck supporting him."

"Then the poor boy will have to learn how to muck out a stall, because he won't be sitting around the house being pampered all day."

Her comment made Abby laugh. "He's going to be cleaning out the barn sooner than you think."

"What do you mean?"

"I found a way to get even with Mr. Dymond without jeopardizing the business."

"Ooooh . . . juicy!" Julia motioned at the living room. "Let's get comfortable and you can tell me all the details." She waited until they both sat on the couch before she leaned forward eagerly. "Get on with it."

"Let me fill you in on how I got the idea, first. You see, Chase purposely invades my personal space every chance he gets." Abby thought about the feel of his chest as he pressed against her back this morning. She stopped to appreciate the feeling once more before resuming the conversation. "It should be annoying when he docs, but it proves to be more distracting than—"

"He's still distracting you. Get to the revenge stuff, already!"

"Okay, okay. When he was all pressed up against me . . . I mean when he was in my space he told me he likes to take a hands-on approach to training—" Julia burst out laughing— "he meant with the horse! Get your mind out of the gutter."

"Only if you pull yours out first. I wasn't the one who started talking about having the guy pressed up against me."

"Can I finish what I was saying?"

"Sure. I guess you told him he couldn't train but you'd let him clean out his horse's stall."

"Not exactly. He had also told me he wanted special attention, for him not the horse. So first I told him he could muck out the colt's stall, and then I suggested if he wanted to be part of the training he could help with the riding."

"Are you nuts? He could get hurt!"

"I didn't think he'd take the bait, especially after he admitted he hadn't ridden a horse in years. He agreed to let me give him riding lessons on Misty and to come in for them at 5:00 a.m. before he goes to the office."

"At least you're not sticking him on an untrained racehorse."

"And I don't plan to. I figure if I give him hard enough lessons for a few days, he'll be so sore he won't want to get on another horse—ever."

"You are evil." Julia grinned. "I love it! I can't wait to see him limping around the farm—assuming you'll let me watch."

"As long as you promise to keep your laughter to yourself."

"I'll try." She leaned back into her end of the couch. "I called the vet and the farrier for you. Doc Hanson will be here after supper."

"Good. I want Lance to have his shots before he passes off any sort of disease to the other horses."

"The poor animal's name is Lance? Talk about calling a skunk a rose."

"Want to hear something even better? He's a stallion."

"You have to be kidding me. He doesn't even have four straight legs."

"Yet someone thought he should be left a stud. I don't get it either."

"Do you think the horse came from Percy Dymond?"

"No way. The man might have trouble picking reliable trainers, but he has a good eye for horseflesh. If I'm not wrong Chase picked up Lance in a hurry so he would have a horse for me to train. If I could prove it I'd get rid of him.

Julia frowned slightly and pulled her legs under her.

"What's wrong?"

"To be honest Abby, I was checking the books and we could use the money."

"Are we in trouble?" An uneasy feeling slithered around her stomach and squeezed. It had taken them four years to get the stable running at the level it was now. She had thought they were finally making a comfortable profit. She didn't want to have to start over again.

"Well . . . it's not the stable that needs the extra money so much as I need it. Things are a little tight for Rob and me since we bought the house. We probably should have saved another year, but the place was so perfect for us and we thought we could handle the payments."

"Why didn't you say something sooner? I don't have much money, but I'm sure I can scrape something together for a loan."

"No, don't. You already do too much. I know you've been pouring your extra cash back into the stable."

"I could just as easily—"

"No. I've found a few independent owners who need a jockey and I've even taken on the odd pony-rider job. Rob's working all the overtime he can get at the factory."

"And you're still short?" Abby was concerned for her friend. It wasn't like Julia to over-extend her resources. She had always been so frugal in the past.

"We'll be okay if we can both keep up this pace and keep the cash flowing in. I don't want you to worry about us, but try not to turn down any clients for a while." She smiled weakly. "Even Chase Dymond."

"The things you make me do for the sake of our friend-ship," Abby drawled, putting the back of her hand to her forehead and falling against the couch arm melodramati-cally. She was rewarded for her attempt at light-heartedness by a kick to her calf and a slight laugh from Julia.

"Like it's so rough. Every second word out of your mouth

seems to be about Chase. You've only known him two days and he's already under your skin."

"I know and it scares the heck out of me. How can I have gone four years with barely a date only to find myself attracted to the one man who is completely wrong for me?"

"And this here is your computer. You do know how to use one of these things, don't you, son?"

Chase resisted the urge to roll his eyes. "I've had to use the odd computer before."

"Good, good. Margaret can show you how to work it if you have a problem."

"I'll keep that in mind," he replied dryly. Margaret was his father's seventy-year-old secretary, who still used a typewriter because she thought the computer was an evil device planted on earth by aliens who wanted to take over the world.

Chase glanced around the professionally decorated office, his gaze landing on the portrait of Georgia that sat on his desk. She stared out from the ornate silver frame, watching his every move. He felt an insane need to turn it face down. Was this woman really his future? What was he doing?

"So Junior, what do you think of this spread?" Percy grinned at his son.

I think it's time to put mom's plan into action. She wanted his father back in the office rather than wasting all his time, and most of his money, on the racehorses. "It's really nice, Dad, but the corner office is usually reserved for the president."

"I know. You'll make a fine one."

"I don't want to be president. I don't understand advertising and I've never run a company before."

"You're a Dymond. Operating this business is in your blood. Besides, this is the family company, you have a greater investment in it than a hired president."

In other words he had a lot more to lose. "I'll make you a deal." He crossed his fingers and hoped Percy would go for it. "You hold the reins as president while I work in operations and get a feel for the company, then when I'm ready I'll take over."

"But I'm retired, son. My horses take up all my spare time now."

"You keep telling me what a great trainer you have. Can't he handle a few days without you there? Or aren't you as confident in him as you claim to be?"

"Mike is the best!"

"So I thought." Chase had learned a few things about business from his father, and one of them was to go for your opponent's weakness. "So, he really doesn't need you at the track all the time, but we need you here." Percy still didn't look convinced. "I've heard some of the employees talking and they seem to think you should still be running the company."

"They won't gain any confidence in you while I'm here."

"They'll be more comfortable with me if I spend some time working in the company before I take it over. At the very least I'll know what I'm talking about when I'm making a decision."

"I suppose you're right . . ." Percy crinkled his brow, deep in thought. "And it would only be until you get a better feel for the ad business. Okay, Junior, you have a deal." He shook his son's hand.

Chase breathed a silent sigh of relief. His mother had been right. Appealing to his father's vanity was the best way to draw him back into the company. It would be far more challenging to find a reason to keep him there, but that problem could be solved later.

"Why don't you get comfortable in your new office and I'll send Terry up to see you. He's the leader of our creative team."

"Don't you want this office back if you're going to be staying on for a while?"

"No, it's only temporary. I'll take one of the smaller one's down the hall. You'll need a nice place to meet with Mr.

Tiessen when you're working on his account. You're going to have to handle him very carefully, son. He has some strange ideas on how he wants his company promoted."

"Oh, great . . ." Chase mumbled as his father walked out the door. He moved around the desk and plunked himself down in the plush leather chair. He spun around in a circle, taking in the room. The entire office was done up in black and chrome except for the light gray carpet and walls.

Earlier in the week, his mother had informed him that Georgia had done all the consulting with the decorator. He wondered if she'd trim a house the same way. It was too stark and too modern for his taste. It radiated the same coolness his girlfriend possessed.

He shivered. Georgia in the office, Georgia at home—no wonder he sought out Abby's company instead. She embodied warmth. The only thing cool about her was the depth of her blue eyes. Everything else was fire, especially the way she verbally sparred with him.

He liked her heat and wanted to get closer to her fire, but it was just as well she wouldn't let him. He'd never had a taste for one-night-stands, or for cheating. He hadn't slept with Georgia, but for the time being he was committed to her.

A hesitant knock sounded at his door. "May I come in, Mr. Dymond?"

Chase looked up to see a slender redheaded man standing in his doorway. "Of course, you're Terry, right?" He stood up to greet him.

"Yes, Terry Lockside. You probably don't remember me, but we went to high school together."

"You look familiar." He shook his hand, then they both sat down. "You were in my history class, weren't you?

"When I wasn't in detention."

He grinned, and Chase could see the mischievous boy was still there. "So how have you been?"

"Probably not as good as you." He leaned forward, eagerly. "I hear you're marrying some hot babe from the south."

"Georgia." He picked up her picture and passed it across the desk. "I should clarify. Her name is Georgia and she's from Texas, but we're not engaged or anything. Just dating."

"Hmmm . . . very blond."

Chase laughed softly. "That's Georgia, very blond. How about you, are you married?"

"Married, divorced and supporting two kids. Do you remember Cindy Neilson?

"The cheerleader?"

"Yup, she's my ex-wife."

"Too bad it didn't work out, she was cute."

"And blond." He winked. "You've got to watch out for them."

Chase laughed. Terry had no idea how true his statement was.

"Your father tells me you'll be working on the Tiessen account with us," Terry said, changing the conversation.

"Rudy is Georgia's father. I don't have much choice but to work with him. I've heard his ideas are a little strange."

"He wants to do live spots with people calling in about their toilet problems."

"Okay . . . weird."

"Tell me about it. No one's been able to change his mind. He rejects almost every suggestion we throw at him. When he says he likes one he slowly transforms it into the live spot idea again."

"He's going to flush our ad firm down the toilet with his idea if we can't change his mind."

Chapter Five

"If you ride me any harder something's going to fall off."

"We're not stopping until you get this right, Chase. It isn't difficult, it's a natural rhythm."

"For you maybe."

"Come on, move with the horse. One, two, one, two. Up, down, up, down."

Abby had been making his horseback riding lessons extra tough. Three days into it and he could barely walk after he got off the horse. The English saddle he was using pinched him and left dark bruises on his thighs. Now she was trying to teach him to post, which shouldn't have been such a difficult task. Rise up when the horse's outside leg moved forward and sit down when it moved back. If only he could maintain his balance as he tried to get the posting rhythm.

The old mare he was riding tripped and he wobbled precariously before sitting down hard on the saddle and pulling her to a stop. If he fell off he wasn't sure Abby would help him up; it would probably be easier to bury him where he hit the ground.

"What's the matter, city boy? Need a break, or are you ready to give up?"

He checked his watch and found he still had a half-hour of suffering to go before the lesson was finished. He wouldn't give up, no matter how she tortured him. "I'm fine—unless you need a break." He couldn't repress the eager note in his voice.

"No, but the blacksmith is supposed to be here soon, so we might as well quit for the day." She walked up to Misty and took a hold of her reins.

Thank God for small miracles! Chase half-swung, half-fell off the mare. He felt like the bones in his legs had turned into jelly. With a concentrated effort he let go of the saddle and attempted to act like every muscle in his body wasn't screaming in agony. He stepped back from Misty and was relieved to find his legs didn't give out on him.

"Are you coming?" Abby called over her shoulder as she walked the horse back to the barn.

"I'll be with you in a minute . . . or five," Chase finished weakly. There was no way he would let her see him limp after her. He would just let his muscles stretch out first before following her. He took off his helmet and wiped his sweaty brow. When she was safely around the corner and couldn't see him, he began to hobble to the barn like a ninety-year-old man with a wheel missing on his walker.

"Hi, Mr. Dymond. How're things?" Melanie seemed to appear in front of him out of thin air.

"Kind of slow and painful." Chase grimaced as he leaned on a fence post near the corral gate. "Your boss is a sadist."

"Playground rules—if she's being mean to you she must like you. Has she pulled your hair yet?"

"No, but I think I pulled every muscle in my body riding her horse. She stuck her tongue out at me occasionally."

"Ooooh, she must really like you." Mel tossed her blond curls and chuckled.

"If this is the way she shows someone she likes him, then maybe I better get her to hate me instead. I don't think I can take much more of her displaced affection." He winced as he tried to lift his foot to rest it on the fence rail. Rather than risk further injury, he left both feet on the ground. "If she's trying to convince me to go away she's beginning to succeed."

"Don't give up on Abby," Mel said seriously. "She's been alone a long time and I think she needs someone to help her knock down the walls she's built around herself. You're the first guy I've seen who's gotten close enough to try."

"You do realize I'm involved with someone else, don't you?"

"I know you are. I've read the newspapers, heard the gossip, but I also know what I see. You don't act much like an involved man."

She was right. If things went any further with Abby he would have to break things off with Georgia. He'd probably lose the Tiessen account. No, he'd definitely lose the account and the family business might not recover from the blow. He wasn't ready to throw away everything he had for a woman he hardly knew.

"I should get to the track," Mel said. "Jim will be waiting for me." She started to walk away but turned back. "Mr. Dymond . . . the secret to Abby's heart is being there for her when she really needs you." She winked at him.

Chase watched her get into her aging half-ton pickup and leave. How could he be there for anyone when he had to take care of his family first? Weren't they enough responsibility?

"Hey there, pokey." Abby appeared from around the corner. "Are you going to come in and unsaddle your horse, or lean against the fence post all day?"

"Sorry, I was talking to Melanie."

"I thought you might have stole over to your car and made a quick getaway while my back was turned."

"How may times do I have to tell you that you can't get rid of me so easily?"

"And yet I keep on hoping." She grinned at him before walking into the barn.

At a quicker pace than before, Chase followed. The aching had eased slightly. "I thought I was supposed to clean out my horse's stall," he remarked when he saw Abby doing the task for him.

"You were late this morning, so I put you on Misty right away. I didn't figure you'd have time to take care of Lance. It's no big deal, I can do it myself."

He'd been late because it was getting harder and harder to pull himself out of bed in the morning. His muscles related their displeasure at his every move. If he didn't get used to riding soon he'd have to crawl to the shower when he got up. He frowned at Abby; she was still loading the wheelbarrow. "You're doing my job," he complained.

"Okay." She leaned the fork against the wall. "If you're going to be crabby about it, then I'll untack Misty and you can do the stall."

"I didn't mean to gripe at you."

"It's all right, you're tired and obviously sore—though you're too stubborn to admit it." In a few short, quick movements she had the saddle pulled off the mare and she was walking into the tack room. "I was only trying to give you a break."

Damn her for being right. She wasn't even mad. "I'm sorry—" he didn't finish his apology as she returned and threw a jar at him. He caught it by reflex.

"Rub this into your sore muscles at night before you go to bed. You can use it in the morning too, but it smells pretty strong. Georgia might not appreciate your new cologne."

He looked at the blue gel then at her. "Uh, thanks. You didn't have to—"

"I know." Abby unclipped Misty's halter from the cross-ties and led her outside to turn her loose in the paddock.

By the time she returned, Chase was almost done with Lance's stall. He pulled the wheelbarrow into the aisle, the old metal frame creaking under the weight. With a grunt of exertion he got the load rolling toward the manure pile.

"I've been thinking," she said before he reached the door. "Maybe we should stop your riding lessons for a while. They screw up your schedule and mine. You could still come in daily to see Lance, but you're clearly not enjoying yourself."

He put down his wheelbarrow and turned to look at her. "Who says?"

"Chase, you've been frowning and snapping at me all morning."

"How do you know I'm not just having a bad day? It's only my third lesson."

"Is it really just that?"

"Yes, as a matter of fact, but you've already made my day better."

"Oh please!" She rolled her eyes.

"No, you did. You gave me some liniment for my aching muscles." He pointed to the jar he'd placed on a bale of hay. "And you let me get off Misty earlier than usual."

"I must be going soft." She half-smiled.

He was confident she would let him come back. "So I guess after I dump this wheelbarrow I'll get going, but I'll be back at five tomorrow morning to see you."

"A promise or a threat?"

"Definitely a threat, because if I don't get the kiss you owe me soon, I'm going to have to take drastic measures."

If these were drastic measures, Abby couldn't take much more. The suspense had her wound so tight she was sure she was going to break. In fact, she already had. In the last three days she'd yelled at everyone around her, including the horses. Fortunately, Lance was proving to be a fast learner, or he would be deaf before she finished training him.

Yesterday Chase had surprised her at the track, causing her to drop the vitamin bucket on her big toe. She had to clench her teeth to keep herself from swearing or shouting at him. Her mood grew ever more foul due to her limp.

"What are you doing here?" she snapped at Melanie as she walked in the barn. "Aren't you supposed to be at the track this morning?"

"No . . ." she said slowly. "It's Julia's day."

Abby smacked her forehead. "I'm sorry, Mel." She felt horrible for treating her employees so terribly.

"It's okay, boss." She grinned at her, never getting upset about anything. "Frustration can make a girl do crazy things. I suspect it has the same effect on men."

"What's wrong with men?" Jim walked into the barn.

"Same thing as the boss."

"Oh, you mean how she wants Chase, but can't have him?"

"You know, I really don't want to discuss my dating life, or lack of one, with you."

"It's okay, boss—you shouldn't be embarrassed. The way I see it you ladies have it easier than the men do. If going without good lovin' were an endurance race the guys would need a handicap."

"Jim, baby, the race is over and the boss won." Mel grinned. "It's time she got her prize, wouldn't you say?"

The older groom snorted. "She should get a prize for working with you and so should I."

Thank goodness Abby could count on Jim when Melanie got pushy about her personal life. After all, she'd only been divorced four years. It really wasn't such a long time. Was it?

"Course," Jim continued, "it wouldn't hurt to have a date once in a while. It might help you relax. You have been pretty tense lately."

"For the last time, I do not need a man or a date!"

"Could've fooled me." Chase walked into the barn as cool and fresh as new snow.

Darn him for showing up during such an embarrassing conversation. He wasn't wearing his sunglasses. The last of his bruises had completely disappeared. He settled his gaze on her and gave her the full benefit of his smile.

"Care to prove your point?" he challenged.

"Put my money where my mouth is?" He was bluffing and she didn't need to prove it. So why didn't she stop herself from marching up to him and taking his face between her hands?

"Is that it?" he taunted.

"I don't need a man," she told him. "And I don't need you or your smart mouth." She tugged him down and pressed her lips against his.

It was only supposed to be a quick kiss. Abby would prove her point and that would be that. She wasn't supposed to notice he tasted like peppermint. His touch wasn't supposed to make her whole body hum with anticipation. She wasn't supposed to enjoy it . . . but she did.

Chase ran his hands up her back and pulled her closer. She didn't need any encouragement; she pressed herself against him and willed the rest of the world to just melt away. She nipped at his lower lip, tugging on it. A soft sigh escaped her and she wished he could understand how he was making her feel.

Gradually she pulled away and looked at him. The real world flooded back in. She was losing her mind! She forced herself to concentrate on her words. "Consider my debt paid, lover-boy, *and* my point proven."

"Huh?" He looked a little dazed. "What debt?"

"The one I owe you for not dumping a bucket of water over my head when you had the chance."

"Oh . . ." He still looked confused.

"Better go saddle up your horse. You're late for your riding lesson and time's-a-wasting." She turned from Chase and looked at Mel and Jim. She raised her eyebrows at them. "What?"

"Nothing!" Melanie blurted.

"You're in complete control, boss," Jim added.

They rushed to do their barn chores practically running into each other in their hurry to get away. Abby walked into the tack room and leaned against the wall. She was not in control. She'd just kissed Chase and not a quick peck either. What a stupid thing to do. To make matters worse, her body was more than ready to do it again.

This shouldn't be happening. He was the last man she should be interested in. He was dating Georgia. His father hated her. Why couldn't her body react like this to someone else? Anyone else?

If Martin had kissed her like that when they were together she would have fought a little harder to save her marriage, regardless of what his parents did to her.

"Abby?" Chase came into the tack room behind her. "Is everything all right?"

No! I just kissed you, you idiot! "Sure, why wouldn't it be?"

"Oh, I don't know." He frowned at her. "Maybe because you just kissed me like there's no tomorrow."

"I did not." She turned and looked at him, putting her hands on her hips. She had to be brazen about this or he'd never give up.

"You mean to tell me you didn't feel anything just now? The earth didn't move? Time didn't stop?"

She looked at her watch and pointed to the second hand. "Nope, still ticking."

"How can you act like *nothing* happened?"

"Because nothing did." She didn't want to lie to him, but neither one of them would benefit if she told him how she felt. "I kissed you, I won't do it again. Don't make a big deal about this. You have a girlfriend to consider."

"This isn't about her."

"Well, it's certainly not about us." Abby watched as his jaw tightened and his gray eyes narrowed to thin slits. He was going to argue with her. Good—she could handle him yelling at her, but she wouldn't be able to resist another kiss.

"How can you say this isn't about us? I wasn't kissing anyone else out there!"

"Because, this is just lust. It can't be anything else," she said, referring back to the conversation she'd had with Julia. He still didn't look convinced, so she tried harder. "Suppose we did get together and you decided to break up with Georgia, your family would be furious. When they discovered it was over me, your father would have a fit. He doesn't like me to start with. You would be alienated from your family. Eventually you would blame me for their distance and begin to hate me. Love has a hard enough time surviving difficulties, lust doesn't have a chance."

"How do you know?"

"I just do." If he kept asking questions she would end up spilling her past to him and she didn't want him to hear it. "I think you should leave. It's probably best not to be around the horses when you're upset." If that were the case, she shouldn't be with them either.

"No, it's probably best not to be around *you*. I'm not feeling very rational right now and I wouldn't want to lose control over a woman who thinks what's going on between us is just lust. This isn't over, Abby."

He turned and stalked out the door, leaving her to wonder what she would do if he decided he was falling in love with her. How could she possibly resist him if he did?

Abby had a point. If it wasn't lust he was feeling then what was it? Chase had only known her a short time. The memory of their kiss lingered on his lips. He could still taste her sweetness and smell her floral shampoo. He longed to hold her long hair in his hands, run the silky, dark brown strands through his fingers. Most of all he wanted to kiss her again and keep doing so until she finally admitted she felt something when their lips touched.

Indecision was tearing him up inside. How could he feel this way when he had Georgia in his life? Sure, she had surprised him with the whole engagement thing, but when he considered it rationally she would make a good wife. She fit the role of the perfect partner for a corporate executive, and Abby didn't.

He drummed his fingers against the steering wheel as he thought. Trees lined the gravel road, their leaves swaying in the breeze. It was a calm peaceful day outside—the complete opposite of how he was feeling.

He pulled into his parent's long driveway and up to the massive white house. It wasn't even six o'clock yet. The rest of the household would still be asleep. He crept inside silently, hoping to make it up to his suite without being heard. He really didn't want to explain to his parents, or to Georgia, that he had had a fight with his trainer because he liked kissing her.

"Master Chase?" Roger's voice echoed quietly down the long bare hall. "Back so soon?"

"No wonder butlers always get blamed for murders, the way you skulk around the house at such odd hours."

"I wasn't skulking sir, you were. Who did you murder?"

Chase grinned at his old friend as he made his way down the hall. The man had a quick wit that never failed to alleviate any situation. "The last butler who became too nosey."

"Hmm . . . I came to work for your parents when you were three. Your terrible two's must have been really bad."

"According to my mother I was Attila the Hun in Huggies."

"I remember. I almost quit because of you and your temper tantrums." Roger turned and walked through the swinging door into the kitchen.

Chase pushed the door open and followed.

The butler reached an aged hand up to the cupboard and pulled out a couple of mugs then poured each of them a cup of coffee. "If you don't mind my saying, you seem to be looking for some guidance."

Chase sat at the small kitchen table, taking the mug offered to him and setting it down. "I could use a whole truckload of advice."

Roger sat across from him and took a sip of his coffee. "Let me guess, you're torn between Georgia and your newfound feelings for Miss Abigail Blue."

"Yes, and I don't know what to do about it. It's obvious I should stay away from Abby, but I can't stop myself from going back."

"What is it about her that draws you?"

He crossed his arms on the table and thought. What didn't draw him to Abby? She was beautiful, smart and more than everything he ever wanted in a woman. "Her great sense of humor, her gentle love for the horses she trains, the way she can't stay angry with me for too long, her smile, her lips, her kiss . . ." He rested his chin on his arms, losing himself in memories.

"Her kiss?"

Startled, Chase sat straight up in his chair. "Did I say kiss? I meant—I meant—"

"You meant exactly what you said. Don't cover it up. I'm old, not senile." Roger shook a finger at him, mock frowning before he broke out into a grin. "So her lips pack a punch, do they?"

"Even more than her throwing arm." He relaxed again. The truth was out. "She kissed the life out of me, then had the nerve to say she didn't feel a thing when our lips touched!"

"And of course you're such a wonderful kisser she should have been falling-down-weak-at-the-knees with the slightest touch." The old man's brown eyes glimmered with contained laughter.

"No! No," he said quieter. "I just can't accept she felt *nothing*. I feel like my whole world has started to revolve in the opposite direction and she says it's only lust I'm experiencing."

"Lust can be a powerful emotion. It's driven many men to do crazy things."

"I am not risking the family business and my relationship with my parents over lust!"

"I didn't say you were," Roger stated calmly. "I said many men, not Chase Dymond. You're far too smart to risk everything you value for a rash emotion."

"You think I'm being impulsive and I should fire Abby as my trainer and never see her again, don't you?" He briefly closed his eyes against a sudden, intense sense of loss.

"I can't tell you what to do, Chase. This decision has to come from you and it had best be soon, before the resulting hurt gets even bigger."

"If it was you, what would you do?"

"I would follow my heart."

"Not the answer I was looking for." He got up and poured

his untouched coffee in the sink. "Georgia's parents are arriving this morning. Her mother is going to go shopping with her and keep her company while her father and I work on his new ad campaign."

"Do you know what you're going to do about this awkward situation?"

"Right now I'm going to go upstairs, take a long, hot shower, change my clothes and hope a solution magically comes to me. If it doesn't, then I'm going shove off the problem and worry about it later."

"Don't push it out too long."

As he exited the kitchen, he wished he could push off his choice for eternity. Silently, he padded up the stairs and down the hallway to his rooms. The easiest answer to his dilemma would be to remain with Georgia. Even Abby expected him to do just that. If only he could convince his heart it was the best solution.

With a great deal of apprehension, Chase walked down the stairs to greet Georgia's parents. Since their flight had been delayed, he hadn't been able to meet them earlier in the day. By the time they arrived, the only thing they wanted to do was have a rest before freshening up for dinner.

He was relieved to see only Georgia waiting at the bottom of the staircase, until he noticed the sour look on her face before she hid it with a demure smile.

"Percy-baby, I've been waiting for you."

He cringed at the name, but no matter how many times he'd asked her to call him Chase she still insisted on Percy. For the hundredth time he cursed his ancestors for labeling their son with that name. "I'm not late, am I?" Checking his watch he saw he was ten minutes early.

"No, of course not. I just wanted to catch up with you before dinner, so we could present a united front for my parents."

"United front? Is there going to be a battle?"

"I don't think so." She nibbled on her bottom lip and cast a doe-eyed look at him. "It's just daddy is really protective of his little girl and he's not too happy I chose a boyfriend who lives so far away. He might be a bit confrontational. He practically had fits when I told him I was going to be staying here with you for the summer."

"So, you're telling me this so I can calm him down and secure his account?"

"I know I've already explained this to you, Percy, but . . ." She patted his arm. "Daddy wouldn't use Dymond Enterprises if I weren't pushing him to do so. He doesn't think very highly of your father or the way he runs the business. He's been reluctant to hand over an advertising account to Dymond Enterprises. I had to plead with him to give you a chance. If you mishandle things tonight, you might not get the account at all."

"And you expect me to screw up?" Already her demands were wearing on him. "Do I embarrass you that much?"

"I don't want you to mention your *female* trainer," she said. "My parents might think there's something funny going on."

"Fine, I won't mention her." He really didn't want Abby's name dragged through the mud when she couldn't even defend herself, and he'd look like a philanderer for trying.

"And could you please try to keep your father under control. One of his outbursts is not going to impress anyone."

Chase wanted to laugh. No one could control Percival Dymond the Third when he was on a rant. "Is there anything else? Would you like me to change my tie too? It really doesn't match your eyes."

"No, there's no time now. I'll help you with your wardrobe tomorrow. Let's go wait in the dining room for our families to come down."

Chase stared at her back as she walked down the hall. Was there anything about him she didn't want to change? He heard voices upstairs and hurried to catch up with his girlfriend. They weren't going to look united if was trailing after her like a lost dog. He reached her side at the entrance to the dining room just in time to turn and greet his parents as they descended the stairs with the Tiessens following them. They stopped at the doorway.

"Mommy, Daddy, I would like you to meet Percy." She smiled sweetly up at Chase as she slid her arm through his.

"Hmmph."

"Oh, don't mind Rudy." Georgia's mother held out her hand to be grasped. "He's just jealous because someone is taking away his little girl."

Chase extended his hand as far as he could with Georgia clinging to his arm. Mrs. Tiessen had long curly red hair and flaming red lipstick to match it. Her vivid green dress was as flamboyant as her make-up. "I'm pleased to meet you, ma'am."

"Don't you know a woman doesn't like to be called 'ma'am' unless she's being addressed by a cowboy? Call me Gloria or Glory, my old showgirl name, anything but ma'am."

"You were a showgirl?" Georgia's nails bit into his arm and he realized he had said the wrong thing.

"Our baby girl didn't tell you? That's how her daddy and I met. I fell right off the stage into his arms when I was performing in Vegas. He invited me up to his room and we haven't been apart a day since."

"Aren't you getting hungry?" Georgia blurted, effectively changing the subject.

"Well, I'm starved," Percy Sr. finally spoke up. He slapped Rudy on the back firmly, eliciting another grunt from him. "You must be ready to eat a horse by now."

"Yes, I suppose I could eat." Mr. Tiessen led the way into the dining room.

Chase noticed he was a compact man with broad shoulders and meaty hands. He had a deep voice that belied his height. Thick blond hair crowned his head and a mustache and goatee covered his face. The entire package was wrapped in a gruff personality.

"Percy-baby, aren't you going to pull out my chair?"

He scooted around the table to where Georgia was standing and pulled out her seat. He'd been so distracted by her father he had forgotten to take care of her.

As he leaned down to push her in she whispered, "United front, remember?" Then she took his chin in her hand and turned his face so she could lay a quick kiss on his lips.

Chase had to resist the urge to pull back or give her his cheek. He was as startled by his reaction as by her kiss. When their lips connected he felt nothing. Georgia's touch didn't have the same effect on him as Abby's. He smiled tightly at her then returned to his side of the table and sat down.

He used to think she was frigid and hoped she would warm up. Now that she was being affectionate he couldn't get away from her fast enough. It was beginning to become apparent he would have to break things off with her, but he needed to wait for the right time. He also needed to figure out how to do it and keep her father's account.

He glanced at the brusque man and got an unfriendly glare back. This wasn't going to be easy.

Roger entered the dining room with the metal trolley he used for serving. He put the food on the table and left again. His quiet exit went unnoticed by most of the people in the room, except for Chase who felt like he could really use a friend in this crowd. Trying to ignore the lion's den around him, he concentrated on his food. He managed to get the first bite past the knot in his stomach before his father spoke up.

"I put Junior on your toilet account, Rudy. He's got some pretty good ideas. We should set up a meeting at the office tomorrow so you can hear them."

"I don't sell toilets, I sell products to clean the toilet. If you can't keep them straight than why should I believe you have a decent idea to sell me? I already told you what I want and I don't understand why you won't do it."

Chase jumped in before the conversation got out of hand and tempers started to flare. "We just want to present you with some different options; make sure you get the best representation we can offer."

"Don't you think this conversation is best reserved for the office?"

"Sara's right," Mrs. Tiessen added. "You boys need to find some better table talk—something the ladies can participate in."

"No offense, ladies, but I won't be interested in shopping—no matter how big the sale was." Percy said.

"We talk about more than shopping," Sara replied. "I mean, really, there are so many things to discuss—like gardening and bridge."

"I'd rather talk about shopping." Chase mumbled.

"That's why I love my Percy-baby. He's interested in all the things that matter to me." Georgia grinned up at him.

Her father graced them with a disgusted snort. He probably thought Chase should be wearing pantyhose and heels. Between Percy's insults and Rudy's inherent dislike for Dymond Enterprises, this was going to be a tough account to nail. Chase slid down in his chair and rubbed his aching stomach. If he came through the summer without an ulcer it would be a miracle.

Dinner was cleared, coffee and tea were served with dessert, and even that was cleared away before the ladies at the table ran out of things to talk about.

"Tell me, Rudy, do you play the ponies, at all? I hear quarter horse racing is pretty big in Texas."

"I think horse racing is a supreme waste of time and money, especially money. I could get more bang for my buck by flushing it down the toilet."

"And it appears you have."

"Now listen here, old man—"

"No offense intended. I was just making a crack about where your money comes from. You know toilets, toilet products, ha ha?"

Rudy continued to glare until Glory started to laugh. "Oh

Percy, that's delightful! You're so clever. I wish I had a gift for word play . . . oh wait I've got one! Sara you certainly snagged yourself a diamond."

"Mother please . . ." Georgia smiled stiffly.

Glory laughed again. "My darling daughter, your boyfriend will love you even if your mother is a little silly when she gets tired. If he doesn't, then you shouldn't be with him."

"Truer words have never been said Mrs. Tiessen." Chase slid his chair back. "I think we're all getting tired and I have an early morning tomorrow." He got up and walked around the table to kiss his mother goodnight on the cheek.

"I suppose you're going to the race track with your father. Georgia mentioned you have a horse being trained there."

"Yes sir, I do." He stared at Rudy, trying to gauge what the man would say next.

"Do you and your father share all the same vices? I wouldn't want my daughter to be spending her evenings alone while you're out gambling."

"Now see here, Tiessen! My son has no vices. He is a normal red-blooded guy, with a taste for the horses. A man has to have a hobby."

"As long as it's only a hobby."

"I don't intend to jeopardize my future with Georgia by gambling my money away on race horses. And I doubt there will be too many nights when she's sitting at home waiting for me." He pulled back her chair. "Would you like me to walk you upstairs?"

As they left the room she squeezed his hand. "You did good, Percy. I'm sure Daddy will come around soon, as long as you keep acting like such a devoted boyfriend."

She had no idea how much he was acting.

Chapter Six

The rusty blue trailer Abby was hauling bumped and rattled from the potholes as she pulled it into the back entrance of the track. She really needed a new trailer, but it would have to wait. Maybe if she had a good season this year . . . of course, she had to consider Julia. Her partner could use a serious raise. Enough to keep the bills paid.

The gate guard waved at her and raised the barrier arm, not bothering to check her I.D. He'd been working security at the track long before Abby moved to Balesworth and recognized most of the trainers and their staff immediately.

She drove past the guardhouse and down the narrow laneway that led to her shed row. She could park her trailer there long enough to unload Lance and put him in one of the empty stalls before she would have to move it. As she neared the barn she saw a tall man waiting near the tack stall.

Chase. She had avoided him for two entire weeks, always managing to be out of the barn before he arrived. Poor Mel had to take over his lessons, but in exchange she got to stay at the barn longer while Abby fed the horses at the track and started morning chores there.

The kiss she had shared with Chase still burned on her

lips, causing her to lose sleep at night and heap huge piles of guilt on herself. Guilt because she kissed an unavailable man, guilt for leading him from his girlfriend, and guilt for enjoying it. She had to face him sometime and it might as well be now.

Abby parked the truck and reached for her seatbelt, when she turned back to her door it swung open and Chase stood beside her. "Hi," she said, at a loss for words.

"You've been avoiding me."

"I've been busy."

"No." He shook his head. "You couldn't have been *that* busy."

She shrugged. "How did you get Mel to let you out of your riding lesson today, or did you go at all?" She'd left orders with her groom to take care of Chase's lessons and not to let him beg off just because Abby wasn't there to give them.

"Did you know she has a weakness for cheese danishes? When I left the barn she had her face stuck in the bag counting how many I'd brought her. She probably hasn't noticed I'm gone." He grinned then, showing her he wasn't mad about being abandoned to the help.

"Oh great, she probably won't make it into the track because she'll be too full of pastry to move. I guess I'll have to use your help with Lance instead. Hope you came prepared to work." She ignored the urge to get out of the other side of her truck and preserve her sanity. Instead, she squeezed into the tight space between the door and Chase's body and looked up at him. "Let's unload your horse."

She started to breathe again when he moved back and let her lead him to the trailer. Together they lowered the heavy ramp. When she had a lead rope attached to the colt's halter Chase released the butt bar.

"Back," Abby murmured softly to Lance. He took a hesitant step back then another until he was standing stretched out with his back legs on the ground and off the ramp, and his front legs still on the trailer. "Back," she said firmly this time, but he didn't move.

"Is something wrong with him? Is he stuck?"

"I think he's afraid of the ramp. The trailer you brought him in didn't have one."

"He doesn't look afraid." A couple of grooms had arrived from one of the neighboring stables. "Do you need some help?" one of them asked.

"I don't think so . . . maybe if I walk him back into the trailer then try backing him up again he'll go." She tugged at the colt's halter. "Come on, Lance," she coaxed. He wouldn't move forward either.

"How about Chase and I give him a push back up on the ramp. Maybe his legs have locked up." Jim had come to join the gathering crowd of curious grooms, hot walkers and trainers.

"Sure." Abby could feel her cheeks warming to an ever-brightening shade of red. She knew how to deal with horses afraid to load, but she'd never had one that wouldn't unload before.

Both men grabbed each others wrists and with no little amount of effort, pushed Lance up the ramp and into the trailer with Abby. "All right, let's try this again. Back up, boy." Gradually Lance stepped back, letting his two hind legs slide down the ramp. Again, he stayed in that position, looking curiously at his handler and the people surrounding him.

A few giggles erupted in the crowd. "He's playing with you," someone suggested. "I'll get a whip," someone else offered.

"No whip. He can't stay like this forever. When he gets tired he'll step down." As if on cue he began to move again. Slowly he slid his right leg down the ramp as if he was moving through water, then as it touched his back feet he moved his left leg. He couldn't remain in his circus horse stance for long. As gradually as he had moved down the ramp he now kneeled on it, looking to the people surrounding him as if he were taking a bow.

Laughter started up around all sides of him and grew into a roar. Lance didn't seem to be bothered by the attention. He got up and shook himself out like nothing unusual had just happened.

"Hey Abby, is he your new star?" Graham stabled his horses in the shed row across from hers. "I had best watch my back, huh?" He grinned at her amicably. Others weren't as kind.

"Please tell me that mangy bag of bones isn't here for training. You're just using him as a pony right?"

"A pony? He's too slow to keep up with a racehorse at a walk!"

The comments faded away as people left to take care of their barn duties. One person remained. It was Michael Dover. He smirked at them. "Nice horse, Dymond. You go to the meat market to find him?"

"Actually I bought him from a friend."

"Some friend." He snorted then turned around and walked off toward the Dymond Dust barns.

Chase looked at Abby and shrugged his shoulders. "I guess he doesn't understand what I see in Lance."

"Sometimes I don't either," she quipped. "Especially after a show like he just put on. I can't imagine what I did to deserve the two of you."

"If that's the way it works," Jim said, "I must have been pure evil to get saddled with Mel."

"Hey! I heard that." She walked up to them. Her blond hair curled in a ponytail at her back and bounced with each stride. "Did you have problems getting Lance out of the trailer? People over at barn 3-B were talking about it when I came in."

"I guess the gossip is spreading fast." Abby said. "Chase's horse was the lead act in the Shady Blue Stables circus show this morning."

"Bad, huh?"

"You have no idea."

"Come on, pain. Help me feed the horses and I'll tell you what happened." The two grooms walked into the tack room.

"Why don't you put Lance in the end stall. It's Aurora's,

but she won't be back at the track for another week. I'll go park the trailer." Abby closed up the ramp and got in her truck. She backed it around the corner and was just putting it into drive when Chase jumped in.

"Are you mad?"

"No, a little embarrassed, but I'll get over it." She pulled onto the laneway. "How about you? Are you ready to sell your horse, get out of racing and back to your doting girlfriend?"

"I'm breaking off my relationship with Georgia. I just have to figure out how to do it without hurting her too badly."

"Why are you telling me this? It isn't any of my business. What you do with your girlfriend is your concern, not mine."

"I don't think Georgia and I are well matched. We don't seem to want the same things out of life. And then there's you and that kiss—"

"It was nothing."

"It wasn't nothing! Why do you keep saying that? You can't convince me there was no feeling in your kiss. You're not so good a liar."

"Chase . . ." She parked her truck and turned toward him, but before she finished what she was saying she found herself caught in his embrace with his lips quickly descending on hers. It was no use trying to fight him; she didn't want to. His kiss wasn't soft and playful. It demanded her full attention.

It didn't matter that he was forbidden fruit. She wanted to eat him whole, fill herself up on his touch, then demand more. His hands felt like fire as they moved over her body, or maybe it was her skin that burned with desire. She left reason behind whenever he was near.

Gently he pulled back, still holding her. "It wasn't nothing."

"I know . . ." Her thoughts were fuzzy and she spoke before she could think out her response. "She may like his kisses, but they had to stop. "Chase . . . we can't do this. *I* can't do this. If nothing else would you respect me?"

He broke off the embrace with a sigh, turning from her to look out the window. "If you really don't want to give us a

chance I'll respect your decision, but you haven't changed
my mind about Georgia. I'm still breaking up with her."

"That's between you and her."

Chase opened the door and practically threw himself out
of the truck. It seemed he couldn't get away from her fast
enough. She didn't want to leave things the way they were,
even if she didn't intend to give him an explanation for her
feelings. "If you still want to continue your riding lessons
I'll give them to you myself." It wasn't much of an olive
branch. He could throw her offer back at her and remove his
horse from her care, but it was all she was willing to give.

He turned to look at her. "I'd like that."

I'd like that. There was nothing else to say. Chase couldn't
have Abby, but he couldn't give her up. So he chose to tor-
ture himself by getting as close to her as he could and not
reaching out to her. They walked back to the shed row together in silence. The tension between them slowly dis-
persed as they got closer to the barns.

"I'm going to have Julia breeze your horse this morning.
We'll do that for the first few times out so he can get used to
the track and the other horses. When he's ready I'll have her
start galloping him."

"Can I stay and watch?"

"Of course you can. He's your horse."

Her response cheered him up. At least he'd be able to
spend the morning with her. As Abby walked into the barns
he noticed the way the sunlight caught her hair, making it
shimmer like a raven's wing. He wanted to pull it free from
the elastic she used to keep it back. He longed to see what it
looked like flowing against her shoulders.

"Do you want to do this?"

He didn't hear her. He was still caught up in his fantasy.

"Chase? Do you want to brush up Lance for me?"

He stared at her dumbly until her question finally sunk in.
"Sure. I can do that." He took the brush she offered him.

"Are you all right?"

"Yeah. I was just thinking." About things he shouldn't have been considering. Abby wanted to keep things platonic and he had to respect her—for now.

"If you need anything I'll be close by, just holler."

"Okay." He needed a cold shower, but he wasn't going to tell her. She might comply. The hose reached all the way down the shed row to the last stall. He was sure she'd only be too happy to use it.

During his two-week break from Abby, he'd decided he couldn't continue dating Georgia. He was still as interested in Abby as the last time they were together. Being with someone else would be wrong. Georgia would have a fit when he broke the news to her. He didn't think even she could remain calm. There wasn't going to be an easy way to let her down.

Lance moved into the brush as Chase stroked him with it. The colt was thoroughly enjoying his grooming. He didn't resemble the horse he had bought *at all*. His coat was shiny and trim with a few dapples showing; a sure sign of how well Abby was keeping him. She had worked off his hay belly, and muscles now stood where there had once been flab.

He finished cleaning up Lance around the time he heard Julia's voice carrying down the shed row. "He bowed?"

"Pretty much. He actually slid to his knees, but he might as well have been bowing to the crowd."

They stopped in front of the stall, Abby towering over Julia. "Hi Chase, I'm here to ride your trick horse."

"Are you sure? He might ruin your reputation as fast as he did Abby's this morning."

"I think I can handle it. He probably won't try anything some other horse hasn't done to me before."

"I thought the same thing until I saw him get out of the trailer this morning. Made me sorry I parked in front of our shed row. Maybe I should have pulled up by the Dymond Dust barns. Your father would have had a heart attack if I parked my rusty blue trailer there."

"He would have called security." Chase smiled. "Probably

would have denied I was his son, and had me removed from his shed row along with you."

"No sense of humor." Abby shook her head. "Makes me wonder where you got yours from."

"You're assuming I have one."

"Oh please, look at your horse. Only someone with the ability to laugh at himself would have brought Lance to me for training. He's showing some potential now, but when I first saw him I had very serious doubts."

So did I, but I was desperate. "You're right. I must get my sense of humor from my mother. Goodness knows she needed one to live with my dad all these years."

"Are you ready for the saddle, boss?" Melanie carried the small jockey's saddle in her arms as she approached.

"Um . . . yeah . . . could you tack up Jess too? I'm going to ride along with Julia in case she has any problems."

"Sure thing."

Mel left Lance's equipment by his stall where Abby could reach it as she fitted it on him. When he was ready she handed the reins off to Julia and went to retrieve her own mount. Chase admired the way she moved so confidently around the horses. She had an ease with the animals that could only have come from spending years working with them.

"My, Grandma, what big eyes you have."

"Huh?" He turned to see Julia watching him.

"I don't mean to be rude, Chase . . . okay, maybe I do . . . but you stare at my friend like you want to eat her for dinner."

"Maybe I would, but her bite is worse than mine. She would rather we keep our relationship on a strictly business level, and for the time being I'm going to have to accept that."

"What happens when you can't accept it anymore?" She looked at him suspiciously.

"I haven't thought that far ahead yet. All I know is she walked into my life and turned it completely upside down.

Without meaning to she has forced me to rethink who I am and who I want to be. For those reasons alone I deserve to know more about her."

"Just don't deconstruct her while you're trying to understand her, okay? I like her the way she is." She winked at him and pulled Lance out of his stall. Jim came over to give her a leg up.

"There you go, feather. Careful you don't soar over the other side."

Chase saw Abby walk Jess out of his stall. He was a ten-year-old sorrel quarter horse she was using as a pony on the track. She swung into the Western saddle smoothly and sat the gelding like an easy chair.

"Texas?" He wondered out loud, suddenly considering the Dallas Cowboys T-shirt she wore and the soft drawl she had to her speech. It sounded a lot like Georgia's, which was probably why he had never really noticed it before. But now that he was wondering where she might have become such an adept horsewoman it made sense.

"What?" she asked him.

"Are you from Texas?"

"Yes, my parents owned a ranch there. They moved to Florida a few years back, but my brother and his wife still live in Meridian. How did you know?"

"Georgia and her parents are from there, too. It just occurred to me you have very similar accents."

"Oh." She looked away from him. "Julia, are you ready?" She urged her horse up into a trot without giving her friend a chance to answer.

He wondered why she was in such a hurry to get away from him. What was she hiding in Texas?

Jim walked over to the grandstands with Chase. At this time of the morning there were only a few owners and trainers hanging around. "We can watch them from here," he said, motioning to a row of seats.

"How long have you worked for Abby?"

"Almost since the day her and Julia moved to Balesworth four years ago. It's the best employment I've ever had. The two of them work as hard as Mel and I do."

Chase leaned back in his chair and watched them go by. They looked like complete opposites rather than a pair. Abby sat tall in her Western saddle while Julia bobbed along at a trot. As they went past the backstretch, they picked their horses up into an easy lope.

Lance seemed to be handling his new surroundings well. He didn't spook much when other horses and riders galloped past him, and he barely noticed the dark shadows cast by the grandstand across the track.

"Your young horse is being a gentleman out there. I wasn't sure what to expect, but he seems quite confident with another horse beside him."

As they neared the grandstand again, Abby pulled her gelding into a walk and let Julia continue on by herself. Lance made it a whole five strides before he noticed his buddy wasn't beside him. He let out a terrified whinny, looking behind him for the other horse. His rider had no problem keeping him in a lope and at the quarter-mile marker she eased him into a walk and turned back to Abby.

They both stopped their horses in front of Chase and Jim.

"I think he's had enough for today." Julia reached down and patted his damp neck. "I don't want to overdo it, though I think he's sweating more from stress than exertion."

"Mel can walk him out when we get back to the barns." Abby looked at the guys. "Meet you back there?"

"Okay, boss."

It took them longer to walk back because Jim kept stopping to answer questions about Lance. He introduced Chase to most of them as the horse's owner. By the time they got back to the barn, Mel was already cooling out the colt.

"How come Julia is talking to Michael Dover?" he asked Jim. It seemed strange, because Abby didn't have anything to do with his father's stable, so he assumed her partner wouldn't either.

"I imagine she's going to be riding some horses for him."

"Why would she? Isn't he the competition?"

"Yes and no. He certainly is to the stable and Abby, but Julia is a jockey so she can ride for anyone. Normally she wouldn't, but she's taking all the work she can get right now."

"Oh." He was unsettled by the fact that Julia was making a deal with Dover. He definitely got a bad feeling from his father's trainer.

Abby didn't like Michael Dover and it had nothing to do with him being the competition. All the other trainers at the track were potential rivals for her, but she got along with many of them. Michael had a way of getting fast results with a racehorse that bordered on cruelty. The animals he trained were often mentally unstable by the time he was finished with them, and they posed a danger to the horses and the jockeys around them.

She couldn't understand why Percy Dymond kept him on as his head trainer. He may be many things, but among them he was always a man who treated his horses well. Perhaps he hadn't seen evidence of Michael's cruelty. She couldn't believe he would still be a trainer for Dymond Dust stables if Percy caught him hurting one of his horses.

Abby vowed to keep her mouth shut. Julia needed money, and running and winning a race for a stable was the fastest way for a jockey to make it. Her friend needed her support more than her advice.

She waited until Michael left her shed row before she approached Julia. "Did he ask you to ride one of the Dymond Dust horses? I imagine it would be good money for you."

"He did, but if you don't want me to I'll back out. I understand the conflict I'm causing by racing for rival stables."

"You're not backing out. In fact, you better win so Percy can't accuse us of purposely throwing the race. Besides, I know our horses come first and you won't be racing against Shady Blue."

"Abby, I would never! I'm jockey for this stable first and foremost."

"I never doubted it." She smiled at her friend. "When are you running for them?"

"Next Saturday, the sixth race. We only have one horse entered in the first race so I figured I would have plenty of time. Unless you need me . . ."

"You and Rob could do with the extra income. I don't need you to help me at the stables, I have Mel and Jim."

"As long as I know you're okay with this." She gave her a quick hug. "You're a very cool best friend. I'll go help Mel saddle up Chi-Chi and then I'll take her for a gallop."

"Good, she's in the fourth race tomorrow so maybe I'll come up and watch you work her. I want to make sure she's not favoring her back leg anymore." She watched Julia walk off.

"You're going to let her run for my father?"

Chase was right behind her speaking quietly in her ear. *Too close.* She stepped forward and turned around, giving herself some needed space. It was too easy for her to lean into him and accept the intimacy he was offering. "Why wouldn't I? I don't own her."

He shrugged. "I didn't think you'd want her working for the competition."

"Everyone's competition in this business. Julia's a good jockey—a lot of stables want her to ride for them. It doesn't surprise me Dover asked her, only that he didn't ask her sooner."

"I don't like him."

"It's Julia's decision to work with him, not yours or mine."

"But you're not happy about it. You don't like him either, do you?"

She shook her head slightly. "It doesn't matter. She still rides for me before anyone else. I don't ask for more. Why are you so worried?"

"I don't know. A gut feeling I guess."

"You're probably just hungry. Maybe you should go home and eat. The cafeteria food here will kill you."

"Trying to get rid of me again?"

Yes. The further temptation was from her, the better. "Why are you still here anyway? We're done working with your horse for the day. I'll meet you at the farm tomorrow, if you have time after your riding lesson we can come here."

"I was going to stay and watch your training sessions with your other horses; compare what you're doing with them to what you're doing with Lance."

"There's nothing to compare. They're way ahead of your horse."

"I promise to stay out of your way."

She regarded Chase skeptically. He'd agreed to back off and give her some space. As far as she was concerned he was still involved and even if he wasn't his family didn't much like *her kind*. She would never be good enough for him in their eyes and after a while they would have him believing it, too.

"I guess you can do whatever you want." Abby feigned indifference. She was disgusted with herself; she wanted the man even as she was pushing him away.

"How about I go off track and get us both something to eat, then I'll meet you at the grandstand. It's where you'll be, isn't it?"

"Yes." *I should tell him no. Send him home.* But she hadn't taken the time to eat this morning. If she didn't have something soon her stomach would start rumbling. "There's a little restaurant about a half-mile north of the track. Their food is pretty good."

"What do you want me to get you?"

"Surprise me."

"I keep trying to, Abby, but you don't seem to like my surprises." He smiled wickedly, letting her know he hadn't given up yet.

She couldn't help but admire the way he moved as he left. His stride was self-assured, eating up great distances with each step. He had on a worn pair of blue jeans, which looked more natural on him than a pair of dress pants.

She had to get over her rabid case of lust, but his appearance wasn't the only thing she found attractive about him. He had a warm, rich laugh and his smile ate her up, especially when he showed his dimples. How could she be so hung up over something as disgustingly cute as a dimple?

Chapter Seven

Chase ascended the stairs to the bedroom Georgia and her mother had designated as a fitting room. She was having a dress made especially for Al's wedding. No one must have told her she's not supposed to outshine the bride.

It was far past time for him to break off his relationship with Georgia. His feelings for Abby aside, he had nothing in common with his Texas socialite girlfriend and their differences were becoming more apparent every day. He still hadn't figured out how to save Dymond Enterprises if he lost the Tiessen account, but at least he was now in a position where he could look at the company's problems and come up with a solution.

He hoped.

He hesitated at the door. The dressmaker was in there, along with his mother and Glory Tiessen. He wanted to talk to Georgia alone. He had to do this now. Their relationship had already gone too far. The longer he waited the worse it would be. He knocked softly on the door, then eased it open a crack. "Can I come in?"

"Oh dear, no! It'll ruin the surprise when you see the fabulous dress my baby's having made." Glory, cinched into a black leather bustier with matching pants, blocked his view of Georgia. "Now shoo, you naughty boy. We'll be done here in an hour. You can see her then."

She tried to push the door closed, but he kept his shoulder wedged inside. "Please, it's really important I talk to her. Now."

"I'm sure whatever you have to say can wait. Just like my Rudy—can't stand the anticipation, can you?"

"For goodness sakes, mother. Let him in. The dress isn't even assembled yet. He won't see anything he isn't supposed to."

"How did a fun-loving gal like me end up with a stick-in-the-mud daughter?" Glory asked, winking at him as she opened the door wider. "She must have got that attitude from her dad."

"Could I speak with Georgia alone?"

His mother gave him a strange look as she squeezed past him through the door. "I should go order the centerpieces for the ladies social at the country club," she said.

"Oh, yes! Sara, wait up. I wanted to know how you feel about sequins. Are they too formal for an afternoon tea?" Glory exited the room and dashed down the hall. Her voice faded as she moved away.

"I'll just wait outside." The dressmaker walked past him and shut the door.

"What's so important that it can't wait?" Georgia stood on a pedestal in front of a three-way mirror. She crossed her arms over the white, satin, full-length robe she was wearing. "I was just about to get into my dress."

She looked like a mythical Greek statue. Medusa, by the way she was turning his feet into stone with her disapproving glare. "We need to talk about our relationship."

"Percy-baby, there's nothing to worry about." She smiled indulgently at him like he was a slow child. "I know you've got a thing for your pretty little trainer, but any day now you're going to realize she's not the type of girl you make a future with. I was born and raised to be the perfect wife for a man like you—a man who will one day soon be the president of Dymond Enterprises."

"All you want out of life is to be the perfect wife? For me? You have no goals, no dreams of your own?"

"You have to admit, you're a full-time job. Why, look at the way you're dressed! You're wearing jeans again. It's not appropriate attire for the president of a company."

He crossed his arms, mirroring her stance. "It's Saturday, Georgia, and I'm not the president of Dymond Enterprises. I don't want to be. I'll have my father back in the office full-time soon. The company needs him to pull it out of the red."

"Oh, that's nonsense, Percy. You'll make the perfect president. You're tall and handsome. You have the presence of a strong leader."

"And I would fit perfectly into your little plan. The president of a company like Dymond Enterprises would surely wash away the past of a toilet bowl princess. Would you still want to be with me if I were only an accounts manager?"

"Why bring up our pasts? We're both better than that."

"See, that's the problem, Georgia. You think working hard for someone else instead of being a CEO is beneath us and I don't. You're more concerned with appearances than I have ever been, or ever will be. We have very little in common and I think it would be best if we end this relationship now."

"Baby . . ." she crooned, stepping off the pedestal. She motioned for him to sit in one of the two chairs. Settling herself beside him, she stroked his forearm. "Sometimes we do things, not because we want to, but because it's the right thing to do.

"How do you think I found you? My parents have money, but their background is questionable. Let's face it, my father is a backyard inventor who got lucky, and my mother was an entertainer." She wrinkled up her pert nose.

"She was a Vegas showgirl. There's nothing wrong with that."

"For common people, maybe, but you and I have to maintain a higher standard. We were born into privilege. We have certain responsibilities to uphold."

"Georgia, you're being a snob." Chase tried to pull his arm free, but she'd become so intense she had stopped stroking it and was now grasping it. "I realize you sought me out because you think wealth and privilege should stick together."

"That's not entirely true, Percy. When we met in New York I knew that we'd end up together."

"We gave it a good try, Georgia. Let it go."

"You came to me when your mother called to tell you Dymond Enterprises was in trouble. You wouldn't have shared your problem with just anybody."

"We were dating and I needed someone to talk to."

"That's not it." She shook her head. "You knew most of our circle of friends couldn't help you, but I could. I think our relationship was meant to be."

"Do you love me?" he asked. He didn't want to hurt her, but if she were in love with him then maybe she would understand his feelings for Abby.

"Don't be silly. When two people are as well suited for each other as we are love is inconsequential. Why, a good marriage is no more than a business transaction and I think we would be great partners."

Not the answer he had been hoping for. "Maybe you don't believe in love. But I do believe in fate, true love and dreams." He didn't know if Abby was the answer to his dreams, but she gave him reason to hope. "I deserve those things in my life and so do you."

Georgia huffed impatiently. "You've changed, Percy. You're not the man I knew in New York."

"I haven't changed so much as I've opened my eyes and seen how good life can be."

"But not with me." A frown disfigured her features. Her face turned red and her mouth opened and closed. She was finally going to lose her temper and act like a normal human being. It was too bad this was the only way he could get her to show some passion. He felt . . . felt . . . five stabbing pin-pricks as she dug her nails into his arm.

"Ow! Georgia, let go." He shook her off and leaned away, rubbing the sore limb.

She jumped up and began to pace in front of him. "It's that girl, isn't it? Your trainer." She spat out the title. "She's the reason you want to back out on me. Have you been having relations with her?"

"Relations? You mean—"

"Don't say it. It's too vulgar."

"Sex? No we haven't."

"Argggh! I told you not to say that word!"

"It's not a bad word. You mean to say you can't even say—"

"Percy! Just because you hang out with pigs doesn't mean you have to speak like them. Stop being so crude."

"I hope you're not calling Abby a pig." His voice held a low note of warning.

"No . . ." A wary expression crossed her face. "Of course not." She stopped in front of him and raised a hand to her forehead. "I meant you're spending a lot of time at the race-track and there are a fair number of unsavory people who work in the backstretch. Not your trainer . . . or her staff, but even you can't vouch for the integrity of everyone who hangs out there." She lowered her hand and stared at him intently. "This Abby . . . you're not involved with her. She hasn't tried to get you for herself?"

"No, Georgia." *She won't let me catch her.* "She is only part of the reason I don't think this relationship is going to work."

Her eyes locked with his. Too late, he realized he had said the wrong thing. But he didn't expect her reaction. She actually smiled at him.

"It's okay if you need to get her out of your system."

He fell back in his chair, stunned.

"I understand a man has needs and if his girlfriend isn't

enough to fulfill them, then he has to seek attention else-where. If you feel the need to have this fling . . . then by all means do it."

Had he been eating or drinking something he would have choked. "Wh-what?"

"Have an affair with your horse trainer, but for our sake keep it quiet, okay? If she protests when you break it off, then I'll go over and let her know she won't break us up."

Her reasoning was so matter-of-fact, she could have been asking him to take out the garbage or buy milk. "I don't want to have an affair with Abby."

"Well, whoever . . . just be discreet about it."

"No, I don't want to have a fling with her. I want a rela-tionship with her." He couldn't believe he was talking about this with Georgia. "I'm sorry, but I won't jeopardize the small opportunity I have with her to stay involved with you."

A muscle twitched at the corner of her mouth, but she didn't frown. Instead, she stared down at him, her face a mask of calm. "You listen to me, Percy, and you listen *care-fully*. If I say it's an affair, then it is—and if I say we're still involved, then we are." She leaned in and braced her hands on the arms of his chair.

"You can have your little dalliance and I'm going to con-tinue acting like nothing is wrong. I've worked too hard be a respectable member of society and I'm *not* going back to be-ing the 'Tidy Toilet Bowl Princess'."

"Stop fooling yourself. We're finished." He pushed him-self out of the chair, forcing her to back up. Before he reached the door she spoke again.

"Do as I say or I'll have Daddy withdraw his account from Dymond Enterprises and take as much business with him as he can. There won't be a company left for you to salvage."

He unclenched his jaw and turned to her. "Don't threaten the people I love, Georgia. You'll be sorry."

She stepped back onto the dress pedestal. "I'm not threat-ening your family, I'm warning you. Call off our relationship at their expense." Her face transformed from sour to sweet. "Now be a dear and fetch the dressmaker for me."

Chase slammed the door on his way out.

Abby rubbed leather conditioner into the bridle she was cleaning. Normally, this would be Mel's job, but she needed to keep busy and keep her mind off Chase. Too bad, her chosen task left her with plenty of time to think. His memory played in her imagination; smiling, talking, riding . . . Chase, Chase, Chase.

She'd seen him almost everyday since he told her he was breaking up with Georgia, but in the past week he never mentioned once whether he had done it. It shouldn't matter to her, but it did.

"What's got you frowning, boss?" Jim walked over to the bench she was sitting on outside the tack stall. "Not happy with the quality of your work?"

"No, I happen to be a master leather cleaner." She smiled at him. "Next to you."

"Good to hear. I wouldn't want you to fire me because you could do my job better than I do. I'd have to move in with the imp and have her support me. It would really put a crimp in her exciting single life."

"I don't think Mel has anything to worry about. Your job's safe. I'd rather be riding or training."

"You don't get to ride much anymore, do you?"

"Who has time? There's too much to do with the clients' horses. The only time I get on anymore is to exercise one of the thoroughbreds with Julia. She does all the breaking out because she's the lightest."

"Do you miss it?"

"Sometimes . . . there are days when I just want to jump on a horse and go riding across the farm and not come back for hours, maybe days. But then I remember I have responsibilities to uphold."

"You need to take a break once in a while, too. You're not a machine."

She shook her head. "We need the money, which means more clients, more horses and less time."

"You mean Julia and Rob need the money." Jim frowned slightly at her. "You can't support the two of them, you have your own life to look after. They're both adults and have to take care of themselves."

"They're my friends. If I can't help them who else will?"

Jim sat down next to Abby and picked up a girth she hadn't cleaned yet. He dipped a sponge into the small pail of water sitting at her feet, then rubbed it against the saddle soap before applying it to the piece of equipment he was holding. "You can't save the world, you know."

She finished with the bridle and started on a pair of reins. "It's only a few extra hours a day, Jim. What difference does it make?"

"And when will it stop? When you collapse from exhaustion? While you're so busy helping your friends, who's taking care of you?"

"The only person I can depend on is me."

"No offense, boss, but that's a load of crap. Do you really think one of us wouldn't pick you up if you fell?" He covered her hand with his and made her focus on him instead of the imaginary dirt she was trying to rub away. "Stop trying to save the world and start living in it."

"As soon as I know the world can turn without my assistance, I'll stop trying to help it." Abby tugged her hand away gently and went back to cleaning the reins. "I appreciate your concern, Jim. But I'm okay, really. If I need support to lean on I promise to ask for a shoulder."

"Just so long as you do," he answered gruffly.

"Hey, boss!" Mel jogged up from between the shed rows and stopped at the edge of their barn. "Julia's race is the next one. Are you going to go watch?"

"She's running for Dymond Dust today, right?"

Mel nodded.

"Yeah." She finished up with the reins and put them down.

"I want to see how she makes out with Percy's mare. The horse looks like a handful. Come on Jim, the tack can wait."

He put the equipment in the tack stall. "Are we going to the grandstand?"

"Yup," Abby answered.

"I'll grab the binoculars." He stepped into the tack room, momentarily disappearing from view. When he reemerged, he handed her the black case before locking up. "Let's go."

They made their way to the front of the track and nodded at the gate guard as they passed him. At the grandstand they jostled for a position near the rail to wait for the race to start. The bugle sounded and the horses and jockeys with their by-riders trotted out onto the raceway.

Julia wore the gold and white colors of Dymond Dust stables instead of Abby's blue and silver. The mare she was riding was already in a full sweat. She snorted nervously and swiveled her head to stare at the crowd, bumping into the pony horse leading her.

"Agitated, isn't she," Jim commented. "I don't think I'd want to be the one on her back."

"Looks like she's already run her race," Mel said absently. She rested her arms on the rail they were standing behind.

Abby watched as Julia was led away down the track. She was a good jockey and there was no reason to worry. But, still . . . Abby bit her bottom lip. The mare fought going into the starting gates until two by-riders pushed her in and slammed the door. "Maybe the mare will focus on her job when the gates open. Some horses fight because they're so anxious to run."

Abby put the binoculars up to her eyes. Dymond Dust had drawn the fourth post-position, right in the middle of the pack. As the last of the horses got into position, the announcer came over the loudspeaker. "They're at the post!" A bell sounded and the gates were thrown open. Immediately the mare dove to the left heading for the inside rail. Julia managed to straighten her out before she ran into one of the other horses.

They raced past the grandstand, the horse finally responding to her rider. Gradually, they moved up through the pack. Abby watched as a spot opened up between two horses and Julia urged the mare through. They held back—pacing themselves, waiting for the right moment to lunge to the top of the pack.

Abby handed the binoculars on to Mel. She was confident Julia wouldn't have any more problems. The horses passed the back barns and the crowd leaned forward over the rail. A steady roar started to grow as each person cheered their horse on to the end. The announcer's voice rose over the noise.

Fifteen lengths away from the finish . . . ten . . . At five lengths Julia's horse swerved violently for the inside rail. Abby's horror increased as she saw her friend topple over, latching onto the mare's neck and hanging there before her strength gave out and she fell to the ground. The riders behind her couldn't avoid her crumpled form.

"No!" Abby scrambled to climb up the rail, heedless of the oncoming horses.

"Boss!" Jim's strong arm wrapped around her waist and pulled her off the fence. "This way." He grabbed her hand and hauled her through the gawking crowd. She thought her heart would beat through her chest as the three of them ran to the entrance that severed the grandstand between the general admission and the owner's stands.

Jim pushed her forward so she could get to the track while he handled the gate guard. The man couldn't stop all them. She got to Julia at the same time as the ambulance; the men jumped out of the van and warned her to stay back.

"If you move her you could make her injuries worse."

Mel and Jim reached her side, both of them taking one of her hands and holding her steady.

"Is she . . . ?" Her voice cracked. Everything inside was so tight she thought her chest was caving in on her. She wasn't sure she would be able to hear the paramedic's voice over the rushing of blood in her ears.

"She's very seriously hurt, ma'am. Are you family?"

"No." She shook her head. "I . . . I'm a friend. Her best friend."

He nodded. "Stay clear, and once we get her loaded into the ambulance you can ride with her to the hospital."

It seemed to take forever. They gently pulled Julia's helmet off her head and carefully put a neck brace on her, then eased her onto the backboard, laying a blanket over her and strapping her in once she was on the gurney. She remained unconscious the whole time. They lifted her through the back doors. One of the attendants gave Abby a hand getting in. She turned to look at her two grooms.

"Don't worry about it, boss," Jim said. "We'll handle everything here, then we'll meet you at the hospital."

"Can you call Rob?"

"Right away," Mel answered.

The man who helped her in shut the doors and showed her where to sit. As the ambulance bumped along the track Julia began to come-to.

"Wh-what? Wh-ere am I?" Her speech was slurred.

Abby slid her hand under the blanket and clasped her friend's. "You fell off your horse. You're on your way to the hospital."

"Can you tell me your name?" The attendant asked.

"Julia Kidd."

He looked at Abby for confirmation and she nodded.

"Where do you live, Julia?"

"1434 Willowbrook Lane, Balesworth, Kentucky, U.S.A."

He smiled at her. "Good." He reached down and checked her pulse then pulled her arm out from under the blanket and checked her blood pressure. Satisfied with them, he put some notes down on his chart. Before he finished they had reached the hospital.

The paramedic who was driving jumped out of the van. He came around the back and swung open the doors. Within moments they had Julia unloaded and were hurrying through the double doors of the hospital entrance. "The waiting room is off to your right," one of them said. "You'll have to stay there until someone comes to get you."

Reluctantly, Abby did as she was told. While she waited she filled out forms and when Rob got there he completed the information she couldn't answer. They held hands, drank coffee and stared at the clock as the minutes slowly ticked by.

"Did you talk to Miss Georgia yet?" Roger was polishing the desk when Chase entered the library. He barely looked up at him as he worked.

"Yes." Chase angrily paced the hardwood floor. He still wasn't quite sure what to do about his insane girlfriend.

Roger stopped polishing. "I assume it didn't go so well?" He left his dust rag on the desk and sat down in one of the leather wing-backed chairs by the reading desk.

"I told her we should break up."

"Then what?"

"At first she was mad. She accused Abby of trying to steal me away." He stopped pacing and looked at Roger. "Then she calmed down and told me to have an affair and get it out of my system. She even offered to break things off for me after I was finished with my fling."

"I think Miss Tiessen has lost her mind. She still wants to be with you?"

He nodded.

"And she thinks you should have an affair to cure what she must consider to be your wandering eye?"

"That's not the worst of it—she threatened me."

Roger raised a single eyebrow. "Really? How?"

"If I don't remain her boyfriend she intends to make sure her father takes his business away from our company and convince as many clients as he can to leave with him. To top it off, I think she expects me to marry her."

"If it were me I'd cut the Tiessen account loose before any damage was done." The old leather creaked as he leaned back in the chair. "You should probably tell your parents what's going on before things get blown out of proportion."

"I know, but Georgia has my mother closeted away with her and I don't know where my father is."

"I think he was going to go to the racetrack this morning. He has a horse running today."

Chase looked at his watch. "It's getting onto four o'clock. He should be back soon."

"Why don't I go fetch your mother and you can break the news to her first, then the two of you can tell Mr. Dymond when he gets home."

"My mother's going to be so disappointed. She really likes Georgia."

"I would think she'd be more concerned with your happiness. I doubt she would expect you to continue dating someone you don't care for." He stood up. "Should I get her?"

"All right. I'll wait here." He sat in the chair Roger had vacated.

Shortly after Roger left, his mother walked into the library. "Is there something you want to talk to me about, dear?" She sat down beside him and examined his face. "You've been acting strangely today. Is something wrong?"

"When you called me in New York and summoned me home I wasn't very happy about it, but I came anyway. I gave up a job I loved and took a position at Dymond Enterprises to help out you and dad. I even brought home a pretty socialite girlfriend for your approval."

"I know all this, but lately you've seemed so much happier. I thought you were glad to be back. The improvement in your attitude came after your welcome home party so I assumed it was your impending engagement to Georgia that brought it on."

"Not exactly. I am happier, you're right, but it isn't because of my girlfriend or my job at the family company."

She sighed deeply. "Is it the horse you bought, or the trainer who works with him?"

"Mom—"

She held up a hand. "I'm not accusing you of anything. I just hope you're going to do the honorable thing and cut one of these ladies loose. But be forewarned, if you choose Miss Blue, you're going to have a battle on your hands. Your father doesn't like her much."

"He made his feelings clear to me when I hired her as a trainer. How do you feel about this?"

"I thought you loved Georgia. She's a fine person, beautiful and smart. I don't think you could find someone who would make a better wife. This other woman comes from an unknown background, she works at the racetrack and I can't imagine she has much money. Are you sure she isn't just interested in your pocketbook?"

"She isn't even interested in *me*, and she refused to work with dad even though he practically threw money at her. She's a good person, Mom—give her a chance."

"You're sure it isn't just a fear of commitment holding you back? Maybe you should take a vacation and really think about your feelings. I'm sure if you do you'll see what an impulsive decision you're making."

"I think you're right, Sara. You're son has already spoken to me about this and I'm convinced he's just nervous about how well our relationship is going." Georgia walked into the room, cool and calm despite the fact she'd probably raced down the stairs to head off his announcement when she realized what he was doing. She stood beside his chair and rested her hand against his neck.

"Percy-baby, it's okay to be nervous about the future. I already told you to do what you need to do to get this out of your system."

"I don't recall asking you to join this conversation." Chase gritted his teeth in frustration. Would the woman never give up?

"Honey," his mother took his hands, "listen to your girlfriend. Don't throw away something wonderful on a whim."

What would it take to convince the two of them he wasn't interested in Georgia?

"Master Chase?" Roger poked his head into the library. "You have a phone call."

"Can't it wait?" he asked.

"It sounds urgent, sir."

He knew his friend wouldn't interrupt this conversation if it weren't important. "I'll be right back." He got up and strode out of the library.

"Who is it?" he asked as he followed Roger down the hall.

"Miss Melanie, from the racetrack."

He picked up the phone in the kitchen, insuring he would have some privacy. "Mel?"

"Chase. Abby's at the hospital and Jim and I had to leave to take care of the horses. She needs a ride home. Can you go get her?"

He gripped the phone tightly, his stomach dropping to his shoes. "Is she hurt? What happened?" He listened intently as Mel explained it wasn't Abby who got hurt, but Julia. Before he hung up the phone, she added one more thing.

"I told you once my boss needs someone to lean on. Don't let her down, okay?"

"Okay." He hung up the phone not knowing what he had agreed to. He sprinted down the hallway to the library, surprising his mother and Georgia.

"I've got to go."

"What is it? What happened?" his mother asked.

"Julia Kidd fell off dad's horse. She's in the hospital."

"Was that your father?"

He didn't hear her question; he was already racing out the door to his car.

Chapter Eight

Abby sat on the edge of the hospital bed and held Julia's good hand. Her right arm was entombed in a plaster cast, as was her left leg. She had been extremely lucky; aside from a couple cracked ribs and some minor bruising, she had suffered no other internal injuries.

"I think you should talk to Doug Eberly about taking over for me while I'm recovering. He's an excellent jockey, and since he decided not to go with Neverwait Stables when they moved to Florida, he's free to ride for us."

"You're out for the rest of the season, you know. And I won't tolerate any arguments from you about it. I think Rob's right; maybe you should consider another line of work."

"The only thing I'm qualified for is fry cook at a burger joint. Is that what you want me to do?" She shifted on the bed and winced. "Damn it!"

"I want you to take care of yourself, Jules. I couldn't bear losing you and neither could Rob." She sighed deeply. "You don't have to flip hamburgers. For goodness sakes, you have other skills. Look at the book-work you do for our stables."

"If you tie me to a desk you'll kill me. I don't want to do anything other than ride."

"I'm going to tie you down to this bed if you don't start listening to common sense. They should have examined your head, too. I think you cracked your skull and your brains are leaking out."

"Quit being mean to the sick person, Abby. It's not nice."

"I'm saving you the argument you're going to have with Rob later. At least you don't have to live with me."

"Thank God for small blessings. Where is my husband? Shouldn't he be back from the cafeteria by now?"

"I sent him home to get a shower and a change of clothes. He intends to spend the night here with you. He's already talked to your doctor about it."

"So I get stuck with you as a babysitter until he gets back," she said sullenly.

"Only if you keep acting like a baby. I'd rather be your friend right now."

"Give me some time, okay. My whole life changed in a heartbeat today. I still can't believe that mare got away from me like she did. I should have seen it coming."

Abby shook her head; bile rose in her throat as the scene replayed itself in her mind. "There was something wrong with the horse. She was wired before you got to the starting gate. Do you think they might have had her on something to give her more run?"

"No, it would be too easy to get caught. Percy wouldn't risk having his stable suspended over something so stupid. I think she was running scared."

"Mike's not known for his gentle training techniques. He expects immediate results from his horses. Isn't Currero his jockey of choice?"

"Yeah. He's as rough as Mike is."

"Don't you think it's strange they put you on that mare if she was already a little wild and hard to handle? If they really wanted to win, wouldn't they have put on a stronger jockey—someone who could force her to respond if she got out of hand?"

"You suppose they wanted me to fall?"

"No, I don't think so . . . maybe they just wanted you to lose."

"But it was their horse!"

"I know, I know. I just can't shake the feeling that someone wanted to see you hurt. I don't trust Michael Dover, and as far as I'm concerned if Percy Dymond has him as a trainer then he's no better than his employee. Dymond Dust benefits if Shady Blue suffers, and without you to ride we're going to suffer."

"I suppose you think I'm guilty by association, too?"

Abby swung around to see Chase standing in the doorway, choking the life out of a bouquet of flowers. "How long have you been there?"

"I asked first. Do you think my family and I are a bunch of dishonest cold-hearted fiends out to get you and your friends?"

"Chase, you walked in on a private conversation."

"It's okay, I might never have known how you really felt about me if I hadn't." He turned and walked out the door.

"Go, go!" Julia whispered to Abby. "Don't let him leave."

Though his callousness was making her angry she followed him anyway. "You don't know anything," she said outside the door. People swept past them in the florescent-lit hallway, either ignoring their argument, or pretending to.

"You're right—I don't—because you won't let me into your life."

"Why should I? You haven't given me any reason to trust you. You're just another spoiled rich boy who wants it all. I don't play second to anyone or anything, Chase."

He frowned at her, his stance menacing. "I told you I was breaking things off with Georgia."

"And you expect me to jump up and down with glee? Throw myself at your feet and beg you to take me?" She crossed her arms, defying all the intimidation tactics he was trying to use on her. They weren't going to work this time.

"It's not going to happen, playboy. I'm not impressed by your money, your good looks, or your charm."

"Maybe not, but a woman who isn't interested doesn't swoon when a man kisses her."

"I didn't swoon! And I may have enjoyed kissing you, but it's not enough."

"You won't let me give you more."

She looked down at the floor, not answering him. "Why did you come here?"

"I came here because Mel said you might need a ride home, but right now I couldn't care less if you had to walk."

"I would rather."

"Fine." He turned and strode down the hall.

"Chase. Wait." She couldn't leave things the way they were, and as much as she hated to admit it she needed him. Not just for a ride home, or as a client, but she liked having him around and she could really use a friend.

He stopped and stared at her. "What is it, Abby. Spit it out fast or I'm leaving."

She swallowed her pride and started talking. "I didn't mean those things I said. Give me a break, I almost watched my best friend die today. I'm an emotional basketcase right now, and I'm feeling instead of thinking."

His stance softened and his frown slipped. She hoped he would forgive her. She really didn't want to push him away.

"I guess I should at least give Julia these flowers before I go."

Abby released the breath she was holding and gave him a tentative smile. "She'd like that. Yours will be her first bouquet, though I'm sure Rob will pick something up for her before he comes back."

"Do you still want a ride home?"

"If you're willing to give me one. Does this mean I'm forgiven?"

"No, but I'll think about it."

"I can live with that."

He walked past her into Julia's room and she followed.

"You didn't kill each other," Julia said. "Maybe you should go back outside and try harder."

Chase moved over to the far side of the bed. "We would, but the nurses told us there's a shortage of blood and they'd hate to waste what they have left on us." He handed her the flowers. "How are you feeling?"

"Like I've been hit by a bus . . . or run over by a stampede of horses."

"From what I heard you were."

Julia nodded. "I was very lucky. It could have been much worse."

Abby noticed her friend's face paled. "Does this mean you're finally coming to your senses? Are you going to find another job?"

"I'm not ready to do anything yet."

"You want her to give up her career? Isn't that a little extreme?"

She faced off with him again over Julia's bed. "I'm trying to lengthen her lifespan. It's not the first fall she's had, but it's the worst one. Next time she might not be so lucky."

"I'm still in the room here, you two!" She looked up at them. "Abby, I'll think about what you said, but I'm not ready to make any decisions. Could we drop this, please?"

"Sure, honey." She sat down on the edge of the bed. "Chase came to give me a ride home. Can I get you anything before I go?"

"How about some water for my flowers?"

She nodded, taking the bouquet Chase handed to her. "I'll be right back."

When she returned she found the two of them talking quietly. She cleared her throat and entered the room. "Could you put these on the nightstand?"

His fingers brushed hers as he took the flowers and set them down. She experienced the same rush every time they touched, and she couldn't keep blaming it on the weather.

There was something about him that made her nerve-endings hum.

She pulled away and leaned in to give Julia a kiss on the cheek. "Do you want us to wait with you until Rob gets back?"

She yawned. "No. I'd like to catch a little nap. Being trampled takes a lot out of a girl." She shooed them out of her room with her hands. "Good night, you two. Take care of my buddy. I don't want to hear you got in another fight and she had to walk home."

"I promise not to kick her out of my car." He put his hand on the small of Abby's back and urged her out the door. "Bye, Julia."

Chase glanced over at Abby as they drove down the gravel road she lived on. She hadn't said a word since they'd left the hospital. She was staring at the trees and the landscape out the side window.

"You're awfully quiet."

"Just trying to figure out what my next move will be. I have to hire a jockey to take over for Julia and help me with the training. I also need to find some extra work to keep the money rolling in, and I don't know where I'm going to fit it into my busy schedule."

"Is the stable in trouble?" This alarmed him. He thought business was booming for her. Why else would she have refused his father's offer to be his head trainer?

"The stable is fine. We're doing really well actually. The problem is Julia and Rob have been struggling with house payments and now they've lost half their income."

"So you plan to do her job as well as your own? I didn't realize you were Superwoman."

"Please don't lecture me about this. Jim already scolded me for working too hard and Julia's mad at me for getting involved in her life. Neither one of them seems to understand I'm just trying to help."

"Fair enough." He didn't want to argue with her again. They were both still raw from their last fight. He wasn't happy about her opinion of him and his family. She carried a grudge against the wealthy that he didn't understand, and until he could get her to open up about it he would remain the enemy.

As he turned into her driveway the sun finished its decent into the west. A few last rays of light kissed the earth before disappearing beyond the horizon. He swung his car around in her wide parking lot and parked in front of her backdoor. "You're home."

The fire he had seen in her when they were at the hospital had vanished. Now she looked lost. She gazed at him, seeming to decide what to do next.

"Do you want to come in? I could put on a pot of coffee."

"Sure." He got out of the car and led the way to her door, taking the keys from her hand and opening it for her. He sat down on one of the stools at the breakfast bar and watched her move about her kitchen. "You look wiped. Have you had anything to eat?"

She turned and stared at him blankly. "Not since this morning. I haven't been hungry." A rumble of her stomach punctuated her statement.

"Sounds like you are now." He got off his seat and guided her to it. "Sit down and relax. I'll make something for you." He rummaged in her fridge, finding very little to work with. "You have two hotdogs, a few apples and half a head of lettuce. What do you eat?"

"Most nights I barely have enough energy to get home and crawl into bed. I don't have a lot of time to shop so usually I end up with take-out."

"Does anyone deliver out here?"

"No." She shook her head. "Don't put yourself out. I'm really not that hungry."

"You have to eat something." He considered the hotdogs for a moment. "Do you have any macaroni and cheese?"

"In the cupboard to the left of the fridge."

He pulled out the box, then found two pots and filled them with water. "It's not exactly fine dining, but it will have to do." He set the pots on the stove and waited for them to boil. While he worked he made small talk with Abby. He hoped the idle conversation would have the dual effect of keeping her awake and keeping her mind off Julia.

"I'd like to enter Lance in his first race in three weeks," she said.

"Isn't it too soon?"

"We're going to run out of season. I thought we should at least put him in a low stakes race to see how he performed, and how much more training he's going to need to get him up to a competitive level. But if you'd rather not enter him, I'll wait."

"You're the expert." He finished boiling the hotdogs and put them aside while he waited for the noodles. "If you think he's ready then I'll trust your decision."

"I don't expect miracles. He'd be lucky to place in the top three. It'd be great exposure for him."

"I have to admit, I'm curious to see how he'll do. I can't believe how far you've taken him in such a short time." He looked over his shoulder at her as he stirred the noodles. "You're a great trainer, Abby."

She blushed at his compliment and smiled. "Thank you."

Something as simple as making her smile shouldn't fill him with awe or flood him with warmth, but it did. He liked having her in his arms; wished she would be less resistant to the idea. Yet, he found he liked just being with her in her kitchen, too. It was domestic, familiar and more comfortable than he would have expected it to be.

He turned back to the task of making dinner, slicing up the two hotdogs and mixing them up with the macaroni and cheese. He opened cupboard doors until he found the plates. Once he discovered where the utensils were hidden, he scooped out two generous helpings and carried the plates to the breakfast bar.

"*Bon appetit*," he said, placing the dish down in front of her.

"Mmmm . . . a man who can cook." She grinned at him slyly. "Every woman's dream."

"Excuse me?" He sat down across from her, his knees bumping into the island. "I happen to be a great cook. The key to it is having food in your fridge. You should try it some time."

"Well, even the best chefs know you need ketchup on macaroni and cheese." She hopped off her stool and went to the fridge. When she came back she stirred a small dollop from the squeeze bottle into her pasta. She held the container out to him. "Want some?"

"No, I don't like to mask my food with ketchup."

She scrutinized his face for a moment then put the bottle down. "You've never tried it before, have you?" She speared a few noodles with her fork.

Chase shook his head. She held the fork out to him. He took hold of her wrist and guided the utensil to his mouth. Chewing thoughtfully he was surprised to find he liked the tangy taste the ketchup added. "Okay, you're right. Pass the bottle over here."

He released her hand and took the offered container.

They ate in silence. When they were done Abby picked up the dishes and headed for the sink.

"Let me do that." Chase got up and followed her. "You're exhausted."

"No, you made dinner, I'll wash the dishes." She looked up at him. "No arguments, I can't spare the energy."

"If you insist." He picked a dishtowel from off the hook on the side of the cupboard by the sink. "But I'll dry."

"You don't have to."

"I want to." He stood beside her, his shoulder touching hers, torturing himself with the feel of her being so close. He watched as she ran water into the sink and poured in some soap. Her hands reddened from the heat and steam rose up to dampen her face. A lock of hair fell loose from her ponytail and he reached over to brush is back for her.

She looked over at him, but didn't comment on the intimate gesture. Silently she passed him one of the plates. There weren't many dishes to wash so they finished their task rather quickly.

When they were done Chase found he was reluctant to leave, but he couldn't think of a good reason to stay any longer. "I guess I should get going." He hung the damp towel back on its hook and rolled down his sleeves.

Abby walked him to the door. She held it open as he stood in the frame. "Thanks for dinner. I probably wouldn't have eaten if you hadn't made it and I would have paid for it in the morning."

"No problem. It's nice to be able to take care of you for a change, instead of the other way around." He reached out to caress her cheek, then bent down and brushed his lips lightly against hers, pulling back before he did anything more. "Get some sleep. You're going to need it."

With the most self-restraint he had ever shown he stepped out of the door into the night, not daring to look back.

Abby checked her watch. *Twelve o'clock.* She had enough time to run home, shower, change and catch afternoon visiting hours at the hospital. Then she could come back to the track for the horses' afternoon feed.

"Are you heading home for lunch, boss?" Mel rested the muck rake she was holding on the ground.

"I'm going to clean up, then visit Julia at the hospital. Do you need me to stay here?" If she had to she could go visit Julia in the evening. It was Rob's time with her, because he worked the day shift, but she was sure he wouldn't mind sharing his wife for an hour or so.

"No! No, we're fine. Go home, take a break, eat something. We don't need you here. We can run this show without you, honest." She flashed her a too-wide grin.

"Is there a problem?" She couldn't shake the feeling Mel was hiding something from her. Maybe I should stay."

"No, boss. Go home." She made sweeping motions with

the rake she was holding. "Go on, before I have to take you to your truck at fork point."

Abby shrugged her shoulders and walked off toward the parking lot, casting one last glance at her stable groom. Mel sure was acting strange this morning. Of course, it was possible they were all a little *off* after the events of the week before. She was sure she'd been asked a thousand times how Julia was doing. Thank goodness she could give them a positive report.

She didn't ever want to experience a scare like that again. It was the reason she was so adamant about Julia giving up her position as a jockey. As her best friend it was her job to take care of Julia and make sure she took care of herself. She wouldn't fail her again.

The trip back to her farm took about twenty minutes. As she drove she thought about Chase and how great he had been at the hospital. He should have made her walk home after the poor way she had treated him.

He hadn't shown up for his riding lessons this week. Although it gave her time to do all the barn chores before heading off to the racetrack, she missed him. The night of Julia's fall he had made her feel safe. So much so that she was able to get a full night's sleep. She would have accused him of drugging the mac' and hotdogs, except he ate it, too.

Had she ever been so comfortable around Martin? She must have—she married him. But as she thought back on her brief marriage, she couldn't ever remember being relaxed with him. Their relationship went straight from head-over-heels-in-love to the arguments and strain caused by his parents' dislike of her. She couldn't think of a time he had been on her side. Not once.

As she turned down her driveway she noticed a black car parked by her house. What was Chase doing here? He should have been at his office. How would he know she was coming home for lunch? She hardly ever did. She suddenly understood why Mel had been acting so strange. She must have been planning this with him.

Abby parked her truck and slid out. She didn't see Chase by the house, so she walked over to the barn. He was inside, tacking up Misty. Jess, who she had brought home for a few days so he could have a break, was already saddled. She looked at him curiously. "What are you doing?"

He grinned at her. "We're going on a picnic. I have to grab the knapsack out of the car and then we can leave. Why don't you take Jess outside and get on. I'll just be a minute."

He brushed past her and she turned and watched him jog out to his car. The wind ruffled his sandy blond hair. She couldn't stop herself from admiring him. *God save me from a man in Wranglers.* She was still standing in the alleyway when he returned.

"Come on, pokey. You don't have all afternoon. Get on your horse."

His statement made her come to her senses. "Chase, I can't go. I have barely enough time to shower and get to the hospital to visit with Julia for a while."

"I won't accept 'no' for an answer. Now get your butt on your horse before I have to carry you over to him and tie you on."

Abby couldn't think of any way to get out of it without insulting him. "Okay, I'm going."

"Darn." He smiled at her wickedly. "I was really hoping you'd pick option number two."

Heat swam through her so intense that she was surprised she could walk to her horse without melting. She managed to keep her composure and concentrate on Jess as she led him outside and got on. She had told Chase she wouldn't be throwing herself at his feet. Right now it was everything she could do to stick to her vow.

She watched as he swung easily up into his saddle. He had come a long way with his riding in a very short time. "What's with the western saddle?" She had been giving him English lessons. "I didn't think you knew how to put one on."

"I heard cowboys make women swoon. So I had Mel show me how to do it when she was giving me riding lessons. It's hard to feel manly when you're perched on a bit of leather small enough to put on a dog. Besides," he paused, motioning to the cantle, "I needed a place to tie the blanket."

He was so pleased with himself she couldn't help grinning. "Where to, cowboy?"

"Melanie showed me this great trail out past the bush line. There's a clearing by a stream out there. I thought it would be the perfect place to have a picnic."

"Sounds like the two of you were having a secret rendezvous, not riding lessons."

"With Mel?" He glanced at her. "Naw, she's too young for my taste. I'd rather be with someone a little more worldly."

Abby tried not to consider the type of woman Chase wanted, and concentrated on her answer instead. "I'm sure she is in her own way."

"Me too, but I was thinking of you, not her, when I was planning romantic trail rides and secluded picnics."

She looked down at her saddle horn. Any witty comeback she might have had fled her mind. She didn't need the complications Chase would bring with him in a relationship and she had no intention of having a one-night stand with him, either—though she doubted it would be just one night. He had been so nice the past week he was contradicting the assumptions she had made about him being a playboy.

"I'm sorry, I didn't mean to embarrass you."

She looked up into his sincere eyes, surprised again by the way he was behaving. *Would the real Chase Dymond please stand up?* "Who are you?" she asked.

"What do you mean? I'm the same guy I always was."

"No, you're different. Why are you being so nice?"

He turned from her and stared off at the horizon. "I thought you could use a break from your life. You've been pushing yourself pretty hard and you had a rough week. I figure if you don't slow down soon you're going to collapse. I'm just giving you a chance to slow down. Is that okay?" He glanced back at her.

"Yes." He was making her feel safe and warm again. She could get used to this side of him. "Thank you."

Chase led the way as they navigated the bush line. She knew her farmland as well as the face she looked at in the mirror each morning. Even though she knew exactly where he was taking her, she was happy to just follow him.

When they got to the stream she watered the horses, then tethered them to a nearby tree. He got the picnic stuff together and by the time she was done, everything was already laid out.

"It's nothing fancy," he apologized. "Just chicken salad sandwiches, some chips and a couple of colas."

She sat down beside him on the blanket, crossing her legs. "Sounds perfect."

He reached for the drinks and handed her one. She helped herself to a paper plate and put a sandwich on it. To say the least, she felt awkward. She didn't know how to take this side of Chase. She bit into a chip and wondered if he had always been this way and she had failed to see it.

"My father went to see Julia this morning. He feels bad about what happened."

Percy's probably trying to do damage control because he's afraid she'll sue him. She barely managed to keep back her retort. Instead of saying something she'd regret, she took a large bite of her sandwich and concentrated on chewing. Rehashing their argument from Saturday night wouldn't solve anything.

"I know you probably think I dragged you out here so my father could make a settlement with her while you were indisposed, but I swear to you, Abby, that's not what's going on at all."

Chew and swallow. Chew and swallow. "What's going on?"

"Between my father and Julia, I have no idea. I hope he's offering her some kind of compensation, but I had nothing to do with him going to the hospital. My reasons for bringing you on this picnic were purely selfish. I just wanted to spend some time with you, but if you'd rather go back . . . I'll understand."

She watched the uncertainty on his face. He was telling her the truth. She would like to go back, but Percy would be long gone. "It would be a shame to waste this food." She took another bite of chicken salad, but didn't break eye contact.

"I agree. It's such a beautiful day out, I'd hate to have to go back to the office so soon." He looked down at his plate. "Mel helped me plan this yesterday. She'll be really disgusted if she finds out I screwed things up by mentioning my father, but I thought you'd want to know."

"I'm glad you told me. I would have been mad if I found out you kept it from me. Besides, you're right, whatever happened at the hospital this morning is between them, not us."

Chase kept up most of the conversation while they ate. He talked a lot about his job at Dymond Enterprises and how he was finally coming to like it. He mentioned the plans he had to bring in new clients and how he hadn't gotten his father back into the office permanently, but at least he was coming in a few days a week.

After they finished eating, Abby stretched her legs out on the blanket and leaned back on her elbows staring at the few clouds in the sky. She should be getting back to the track, but her conscience didn't seem to care and she wasn't ready to jump back into reality yet.

"Don't do that," he rumbled.

"What?" She glanced at him. "Breathe?"

"Yes. I had no intention of bringing you out here to seduce you. But even watching you breathe gets to me." He got up onto his hands and knees and crawled over her. "I didn't bring dessert, but I can think of another sweet way to finish our meal."

He put his hands on either side of her arms and she looked up at him. She thought she should stop this before it went any further, but her limbs seemed to have turned to liquid. All she wanted him to do was lean forward and kiss her.

Slowly he began to lower his head, never taking his eyes

from hers. She felt his warm breath caress her lips and let her lids flutter closed. The barest touch of his mouth and she heard ringing.

"Dammit! I should have left my cell phone in the car."

Her eyes snapped open as it rang again. "Aren't you going to get it?"

He sat back on her legs, pinning her under him. "I guess I should." He reached for the phone and flipped it open. "Hello?"

"Theo? I'm busy right now can I call you—"

"Well, actually Lance is my horse now, but yes, he's fine." Chase winked at her. "You bought a cookie factory? Why are you calling me?"

"Oh!" He glanced at Abby, then lifted himself off her legs and sat beside her, playing with the fingers on her left hand. "You want me to meet you at the office so we can discuss an advertising budget and options? I can schedule you in tomorrow—"

"I guess if you're leaving for Sweden tomorrow we'll have to get together this afternoon. Why are you going to Sweden?"

"A chocolate factory probably would save on the cost of buying chocolate chips, and real Swiss chocolate would be a great selling angle, you're right."

"Okay . . . bye, Theo. I'll meet you at the office in an hour."

He took her hand and stood up, pulling her with him. "Sorry Cinderella, it's midnight and your prince just turned into a pumpkin. I have to get back to the office."

"Seems to me the coach was the pumpkin." She eyed him up and down. "Besides, Prince Charming is a bit of a stretch for you. Most of the time you act more like Georgie Porgy."

"You are so lucky I don't have time to finish this." He gave her a quick peck on the lips. "But I have a long memory and you're going to have to pay for the insult."

Chapter Nine

On race day the track hummed with activity. Chase just managed to avoid being run down by a passing stable groom with her arms full of blankets. He dodged horses, hotwalkers, trainers and jockeys as he steadily made his way to the Shady Blue barn.

He'd barely seen Abby in the two weeks since their picnic. He knew she was avoiding him again, but he was so caught up in the deal he was putting together for Theo he couldn't spare the time to track her down.

Last night he had finally agreed on an advertising plan with Terry. He could understand why the man was the head of the creative department; he had more ideas than Chase could keep up with. Together they had managed to assemble a strong ad campaign for the cookie factory's "Swiss Chips" line. If they could sell it to Theo, then Chase wouldn't need to worry about losing the Tiessen account. He'd finally be free of Georgia.

As the barn came into view he saw Jim and Melanie bustling about, but no sign of their alluring boss. He slowed his pace down and watched the activity around the barn.

"Hey there, Mr. Dymond. Are you excited about Lance's first race?" Mel waved to him from his horse's stall.

" 'Apprehensive' would probably be a better word." He stopped at the stall door and looked in.

She had gone back to grooming the colt, but turned to respond to him. "Abby seems to think he's ready. I guarantee she wouldn't have had you enter him if she didn't."

"Where is your boss anyway? Shouldn't she be here overseeing things?" He glanced around, but still didn't see her.

"Mmmm . . ." Mel gave him an assessing look. "Maybe you're more excited to see Abby. How did your picnic go? She won't tell me what happened."

"Then you're going to have to keep guessing, because my lips are sealed. So . . . where's your boss?"

"She went to round up Eberly. He'll be riding Lance for you." She began brushing the colt again. "She should be back soon."

Chase gave up on Mel; he wasn't going to get any more information on Abby's whereabouts from her. He wandered over to the bench placed in front of the tack stall and sat down to wait. After a bit Jim came and joined him.

"Waiting on the boss?"

"Yeah." He leaned forward and rested his elbows on his knees. "In more ways than one."

"Won't let you get too close will she? Doesn't surprise me really. I imagine she doesn't want to make the same mistake twice, though I doubt you're much like her Martin had been. If you were, you would have given up by now and resorted to spreading nasty rumors about her."

"Who's Martin?" Chase gave his full attention to the man beside him, intent on absorbing this glimpse into Abby's past.

"Her ex-husband. A real player from what I understand. Learned how to manipulate people from his family. His parents tried to control his every move." Jim paused and looked at him. "This information stays between you and me. I won't have the boss thinking I betrayed her."

"Why are you telling me this?"

"Because I hate to see her alone. She works so hard at taking care of us and she has no one to do the same for her. I wouldn't say anything at all except you seem to look at her with the same longing in your eyes that she has when she's watching you."

"So you think—"

"I think I'm a gossiping old man who should mind his own business, but can't." He got up to leave. "By the way, the boss is on her way." He pointed at Abby, who was coming down the dirt lane with a short, tanned, dark-haired man.

She waved as she approached and Chase saw none of the hesitancy he had expected in her. She wasn't acting like she was avoiding him, but he was sure she had been. He stood up as they arrived at the barn.

"Chase, I'd like you to meet Doug Eberly." She looked back and forth between the two men. "He's going to be riding your horse today."

They shook hands and he marveled at the strength in the small man's hand.

"I have a spare set of silks in the tack room. I brought them from home this morning. Be right back." She slid past Chase into the converted stall.

"So you're the man who owns the trick horse?"

"Yeah, that's me, and Lance is my traveling sideshow."

"Don't be too hard on him. I've seen him work the past couple of weeks and he's doing well for an inexperienced colt. He's got one hell of a stride on him."

"Here they are." She handed the blue and silver jacket and helmet cover to him. "I hope they fit. This set was a little big on Julia so I kept it aside in case someone else had to ride for us."

Doug slipped on the silky jacket, snapped it up and swung his arms around in it. "Feels all right to me. Thanks Abby, I'll see you at race time." He walked off the way he had come.

"Seems like a nice enough guy."

"He is," she said absently. "He's a good jockey, too. We were lucky to get him before anyone else snatched him up."

She glanced at Chase and he noticed the wary expression on her face. She'd been so warm the day of the picnic he thought he had finally broken through her defenses, but now he found she had raised the walls against him again. "We need to talk," he said.

"I don't want to." She moved past him toward the other end of the barn. "I had better check on Mel—see how she's making out with Lance."

He stopped her mid-stride. "Abby, I don't get it. Don't you trust me?

"I don't trust me. Okay? I didn't even want to stop you the other day. If your phone hadn't started to ring . . ." She shook her head. "I like my life the way it is. It's simple and you're one huge complication messing it up on me."

"You can't keep your heart in a box on the shelf, you know."

"You can't stop me from trying." She pulled her arm away and glared up at him.

"Who am I to resist a challenge?" He smiled, putting all his intentions into it. He respected her need for space, but he wouldn't accept her keeping him away because she was afraid to try. "I'm going to go look in on my horse. You coming?"

Turning, he made his way to Lance's stall. She had caught up to him before he reached the door. "Chase . . ." she hissed. "We aren't finished."

"You don't want to talk, remember?" He noticed the way a muscle in her jaw ticked when he taunted her. "Of course, if you've changed your mind we can find someplace quiet to finish this discussion."

Mel chose that moment to leave the stall. "Something wrong?"

"No." Abby stepped away from him. "Everything's fine. Is Lance ready?"

"I'm just going to get his tack." She pushed between them. "Be back in a jiffy!"

"Liar." He leaned in and whispered in her ear, enjoying her warmth and nearness.

"Pain in the rump," she retorted, stepping into the horse's stall to inspect him herself. Chase moved to follow her, but she held her hand up. "You stay out there while we're working."

She managed to keep him at the same distance for the rest of the hour as they prepared for Lance's race. Finally she exiled him to the grandstand by himself to wait out the race. He wasn't happy about his banishment, but he could hardly argue with her about it. She was the trainer and her orders were meant to be followed.

He avoided his family's owner's box on the off chance his father would be there. Instead he stood by the railing staring at the backstretch, hoping he might catch a glimpse of Abby. *What's wrong with me?* He needed to get a life, one that didn't revolve around the tall, sable-haired beauty hiding out at the barns. When had his every thought begun to circulate around her?

The answer disturbed him. From the moment he met Abby she had dominated his thoughts. He was clearly doomed to follow this course until the end, or until she tossed him out of her life. His heart squeezed painfully with the notion. Although he had only known her a short while, he couldn't imagine not having her to spar with.

Abby watched Mel pull Lance out of his stall as she sent a little prayer up to heaven. It wasn't a wish for him to win the race, or even place in it; she just didn't want him to embarrass her stable. *Please, God, don't let this be a big mistake.* If it were she'd kill Chase for all the pain he had caused, including the turmoil he set off in her body whenever he was near.

She had to send him away so she could concentrate. It was easier to deal with his horse than him. Lance wasn't as persistent as his owner when it came to getting his way. He didn't back her into corners, offering her no escape.

"Do you want me to bring the colt up front or would you rather do it yourself this time?" Mel asked.

"I'll follow you. Doug will meet us there." Abby turned and glanced around herself, spotting Jim. "You coming?"

"I've got a couple of things to finish here before post-time so I'll just watch from the backstretch."

"Suit yourself." She shrugged. "Let's go, Mel. Doug's waiting."

She followed her groom and the horse to the viewing area where spectators and dedicated gamblers flocked to see the horses before the race. She spotted her jockey standing by stall number three, Lance's post-position.

Mel backed the colt into the wide-standing stall and started her last minute check of his equipment. He stood quietly, watching the activities around him while she tightened the girth and put on his bridle.

"He's pretty calm." Doug nodded at the horse. "You sure it's his first race?"

"Oh, it's his first all right. I'd be worried he wasn't going to run except he's been this sedate through the whole training process. Nothing seems to bother him."

"Riders up." The signal was given to have the jockeys mount their horses. The handlers would then led them onto the landscaped circle where the spectators could view them before the race began.

Mel held onto Lance's head as Abby gave Doug a leg up. She waited until he was firmly in the saddle before walking into the circle. When the signal was given, Mel lead the pair to their waiting pony rider.

With a silent wave of good luck, Mel and Abby watched them disappear under the archway that led to the track. They wove through the crowd to the grandstand and found Chase standing near the rail waiting for them.

"This is it," he said. "You nervous?" He twisted a racing program in his hands, staring at her anxiously.

"No. He'll do fine. No one's expecting him to win."

He nodded at her before turning back to the track.

Abby leaned in beside him to watch Lance being loaded into the gate. She was far more nervous than she had admitted to Chase. Every time one of her horses went out her reputation was on the line. She was afraid any mistake they made would look bad on her, whether that was the case or not.

She glanced at Chase and noticed he was watching her. Was he anxious about his horse or her? "What?" She finally blurted when she couldn't take his intense scrutiny anymore.

"Nothing."

"That was not a 'nothing' look. What is it? You think Lance is going to screw up, don't you? You think I'm an awful trainer and I was crazy to enter your horse in a race so soon."

"I was wondering if you would go to the Horseman's Ball with me."

"Oh—" She was about to say more, but the gate buzzer sounded.

"They're off!" The announcer shouted at the crowd.

Lance launched out of the gate straight and true without swerving into the other horses or giving up any ground when one of them bumped into him. He successfully fought to keep his place in the pack, staying in the middle.

"Is he doing good? Shouldn't he be at the front?" Chase leaned over the rail.

"Doug's got him right where he should be. If he sends him to the front right away he might tire out and drop to the end of the pack before the race is over."

At the half-mile marker horses began shifting positions. Some of them fell back while others made a rush for the front. Lance continued to hold the same place, fourth horse back. They came around the final bend without losing any ground.

People stood in the stands shouting at their designated winner, pushing them on with the strength of their will. Ten lengths from the end Lance put on a burst of speed. He began to push through the pack. Third place . . . second . . . and nose-to-nose for first at the finish.

"It's a photo finish!" The announcer shouted over the

crowd. "Please hold onto your tickets until we receive the official judgment."

Chase grabbed Abby up in a fierce hug and let out a loud whoop. He swung her around and gave her a resounding kiss on the lips. "Did you see that? My horse did that. The circus horse. He came out of nowhere and ran straight for the front."

"I know. I saw!" She steadied herself as he set her down and took Melanie into his arms. "Lance hasn't won it yet, we have to wait for the results."

"Who cares?" He let go of the groom. "He wasn't supposed to place at all."

"I'll go meet up with Doug and Lance. Maybe you two should wait for us by the winner's circle." Mel winked. "Just in case."

"Did you know he was going to do this?"

"I knew he could, but I never expected him to do so well in his first race." She shrugged her shoulders.

"Ladies and gentlemen," the announcer interrupted. "We have the results from the fifth race. It's Lancelot's Mighty Sword to win. Carlito's—"

Abby didn't hear the rest over her own amazement and Chase's excitement. "I can't believe he did it," she mumbled. "I guess we better get over to the winner's circle to have our picture taken. I'm sure you'll want one, since it's his first win."

"Lead the way." He grinned at her.

They wove quickly through the throngs of people and over to the gate, showing their badges to be allowed admittance. Mel and Doug were waiting for them there.

"Congratulations!" She shook her jockey's hand. "That was one hell of an impressive ride."

"To be honest, Lance did all the hard work. He trusted me completely out there. When I asked him to make a move, he did." He turned and looked at Chase. "I sure enjoyed riding him, Mr. Dymond. I hope I'll get another chance."

"I'm okay with it if Abby is."

She nodded. "I hope you'll ride some of my other horses too, Doug. I've got a stable full."

"You bet. Especially if they're like my buddy Lance here." He gave the big colt a hearty pat on the neck.

"Okay, folks." The photographer interrupted. "I'm ready when you are. Just get yourselves organized and I'll take the picture."

Mel held Lance's head and Doug stood beside her. Chase took up the next position with his arm wrapped tightly around Abby. He looked down at her and she was instantly lost in his gaze.

"Smile!"

She tore her eyes away from his and grinned at the camera, hoping it didn't look like a grimace. Her feelings for the man beside her were getting more complicated all the time. He wasn't an opponent, an obstacle, or a means to an end—and he wasn't a friend. So what was Chase becoming to her?

Chase was walking on air. Okay, it was just a little race and the competition wasn't all that tough, but his horse won! Abby was clearly the best trainer in the world and he intended to tell her so as soon as he got the chance. Since they got back to the barns he hadn't had a quiet moment alone with her.

He wanted to talk to her about more than just Lance. She hadn't answered whether or not she'd go to the Horseman's Ball. It was suddenly imperative she did, and not just because she was his trainer, either. If people saw them walk into the country club together then their relationship might be more real. If they saw them dancing together they might wonder if something more was going on. If they saw him holding her hand then they might talk. And if they believed he was interested in Abby then maybe she would finally start to believe it, too.

"So how do you feel about all this?" Jim asked, walking up to him from around the corner.

I feel like begging your boss to have mercy on me. I feel like kissing her until she gives in and lets me get closer to her. "I'm a little stunned Lance did so well, but other than that I feel great." He groaned internally. He felt frustrated, confused and annoyed, more than he felt great.

"I didn't realize your colt had so much heart. He really surprised me—and a few other people, I suppose."

Chase spotted Abby over Jim's shoulder as she walked into the tack stall. She was finally alone. Doug was gone and Mel was preoccupied with Lance. "Could you excuse me? I wanted to talk to your boss about something."

"That's not a 'talk' look you have on your face. It's an 'action' look."

He grinned, striding past the groom into the tack stall.

"Abby?" He heard her quick intake of breath as she dropped the feed bucket she was holding.

"Damn." She stooped to pick it up. "I've dropped more things since I've met you." She turned and glared at him. "Quit sneaking up on me."

"I never do." Then he let his voice take on an arrogant swagger. "Maybe you're so overwhelmed by my presence you can't control your actions."

She fired a cotton bandage at his head. It bounced off harmlessly. "Oh . . . guess you're right." A Cheshire grin covered her face.

Chase laughed at her smug expression. His Abby never let him get the better of her for long. *His Abby? Where had that come from?*

"Did you just come in here to bug me, or is there something you need?"

"You." He advanced on her. "I need you. Drop the bucket and anything else you might hit me on the head with and come over here." To his astonishment, she did as he said.

Before she could change her mind he swung her around

him in a joyous hug and gave her an exuberant kiss on the lips. "He did it! Can you believe it?"

"I know." She hugged him tightly, her feet dangling over the floor. "He ran like a pro. I wish we had videotaped it."

He let her slide down his body, but she didn't step away. Instead, she put her hands on his cheeks and kissed him again. This time it wasn't celebratory. She took possession of his lips.

Chase lost himself in her touch. He was drowning. Her teeth tugging on his bottom lip was like an undercurrent pulling him down, and her warm breath was the sea drawing him deeper. One last gasp of air and he let himself sink into her. He opened his mouth and she invaded him with her tongue and her sweet taste. She wasn't close enough. He wanted to be a part of her.

"Chase . . ." she whispered into his mouth, stepping back, but pulling him with her away from the door. "Your timing sucks." Still she didn't stop kissing him. "I've got chores to do." She licked the corner of his mouth. "Mel or Jim could walk in at any moment . . ." She pressed her lips full against his.

"Ask me if I care," he growled before tangling his tongue with hers. Beneath his desire there was a need to brand her as his. He tried to show her what he couldn't say. She was his, no matter how hard she tried to deny it.

A rake clattered to the ground outside. Chase came quickly back to his senses, remembering they weren't really alone. "Maybe we could continue this later?"

Abby looked up at him and groaned. "No . . . we shouldn't have started this." She pulled out of his arms. "Oh God, what am I doing? We're horrible for each other." With a sigh she began to pace the small room. "There is no *us*," she said firmly, not looking directly at him. "And there is definitely no more kissing."

"I'm not allowed to kiss you anymore?" He weighed her resolve as he watched her stare at his lips.

"No . . . more . . . kissing . . ."

Chase smiled at her. She didn't sound like she believed her convictions too deeply. "If you say so." He shrugged.

She snapped her gaze up to his. "I do."

For now. "You never answered my question before."

"What question?"

"I asked you if you'd go to the Horseman's Ball with me at the country club before Lance's race started."

"Oh . . . well . . ." She grimaced. "I appreciate the gesture, but it's not my type of crowd. I never go to those things. They're far too formal for me."

"But you have to go with me now. Lance won! I want to show off the best trainer this side of Kentucky has ever seen."

She shook her head. "Caviar gives me indigestion."

"I promise not to make you eat it. There'll be other trainers attending."

"They like to schmooze, I don't."

Chase had another reason for her to go. "You need to schmooze to get more clients so you can take care of Julia. If you won't go for me, do it for her."

"For Julia?"

He nodded, seeing she was about to cave. "Please."

"All right." She sighed. "It's only one night. How bad could it be?"

"This is horrible!" Abby burst through Julia's bedroom door. "I kissed him again." She sat on her friend's bed, careful not to jostle her.

The doctors had released her after a week and a half in the hospital, feeling she would get a better rest at home. There wasn't much else they could do other than give her time to heal.

"I assume you're talking about Chase."

"Yes. This makes at least three times already."

"Only three? You have nothing to worry about."

"What do you mean? I wasn't going to do it once!"

Julia shifted up against her pillows and laughed. "Abby,

you can still count on one hand how many times you've kissed him. You don't have a problem until you lose track."

"But I *like* it." And feeling anything for Chase was dangerous. He would tear her world apart if he dumped her, and eventually she would run out of racetracks to disappear to.

"Thank goodness." Julia smiled. "I was beginning to think you were made of ice. I have Rob and even I would have to look twice at a man like Chase if he was throwing himself at me."

"He is not."

"Honey." Julia took her hand. "I'm surprised you haven't been flattened. If the guy tries much harder he's gonna hurt himself."

Abby thought about how great he had been since her friend's fall. Maybe he was trying to show her he cared. But if that were the case then she was in real trouble, because she didn't think she could resist him if he sincerely liked her.

"How'd it happen, anyway?"

"Huh?"

"The kiss."

"Oh . . . it started out as an 'I'm-happy-my-horse-won' kiss and then it got out of control."

"Whoa!" Julia held up a hand. "Back up. Did you just say *Lance* won his race?"

"Yeah, I forgot to tell you. He won. It was great. I kissed Chase."

"It must have been one hell of a kiss if the news about his horse came second in your list of priorities." She laughed. "Was it good?"

"Sweet as an overripe peach, and as hot as black leather in the summer sun."

"Mmmm . . ." Julia smiled. "Sounds as if you liked it."

"I don't think I would stop him from doing it again."

"What about his girlfriend?"

"He said he was going to break things off with her a few weeks ago, but he hasn't said anything about it since. You don't think he's still involved with her, do you?"

She shrugged. "I guess you'll have to ask him."

Abby bit her lip. Chase had all the characteristics of a seasoned player. She didn't doubt his time in New York was spent with many different women. What if she was just a challenge to him? Would he have his fun with her then choose Georgia instead?

These weren't answers she'd find in Julia's bedroom, so she changed the topic. "How are you doing? Everything healing all right?"

"The doctors seem happy with my progress. I can't move around on my own yet. I don't know what I'd do without Rob." She frowned. "I just wish . . ."

"What is it?" She leaned in and gave her friend her full attention. "Is something wrong?"

"Abby, I didn't want to say anything because I didn't want to worry you, but Rob lost his job."

"Oh no."

"His boss told him he'd been off work too much this past week and instead of letting him take a leave of absence he fired him. He's not union or anything, so there's no one to fight for us and we can't afford legal fees on top of the medical bills. I don't know what we're going to do."

"I'm sure he'll find something else and in the meantime he can work for me. I've been thinking about expanding my clientele—"

"I don't want you to feel you have to take care of us. We'll find a way . . . if only we didn't have these stupid house payments."

"I'm going to the Horseman's Ball." She held her breath and waited for a response. Only Julia understood her aversion the event.

"Because of me?"

"Mostly. Chase asked me to go with him. He said it would be a good place for me to make more contacts, maybe even meet a few potential clients."

"I know how uncomfortable you feel in a room full of rich people, but they're not all like Martin's parents. They're not better than you because of their wealth and most of them know they're not."

Abby nodded. "It's about time I got over the Blue's snub." She sighed deeply. "I'm going to do this."

"All right, now let me be your fairy godmother." Julia snuggled down into her pillows. "Do you still have your low cut black dress?"

"It's in the back of my closet, along with a dozen other things I'll never wear."

"Well pull it out and dust it off, because it's perfect and it's going to make Mr. Chase Dymond drool. If he hasn't dumped his girlfriend yet, he will after he sees you in it."

"That's horrible!"

She shrugged. "Maybe, but I happen to think it's true. Of course, if you don't want his attention then by all means wear one of your pantsuits. How about the dowdy green one? It makes you look like a giant string bean."

Abby stuck out her tongue. "I donated it to the Salvation Army after the first time I wore it. You really think I should wear the black one?"

"Trust me, it's the perfect dress. If you'd worn it to your divorce hearing, Martin would have begged you to stay with him and you would have gotten a much better deal."

"I didn't want any of his money. I don't need hand-outs from anyone; I can take care of myself," she ground out.

"Easy there, Superwoman. I was kidding."

She relaxed again, getting back into their conversation. "Which shoes should I wear?"

Abby left after lunch. She was still apprehensive over the ball, but at least she had a plan. As she drove down Julia's road she checked in the rearview mirror. Before the house disappeared from sight she noticed a navy blue Mercedes pulling into the driveway. What was Percy Dymond doing there?

Chapter Ten

A loud crack of thunder rattled the windows of the small house as Abby attempted to get ready for the party. How was she ever going to get through tonight? She had to make nice with Chase's family, friends and associates—all in the pursuit of new clients, all for Julia.

While she attempted to be professional and not make a fool out of herself Julia would be lying in her bed waiting for some good news. Her medical bills weren't getting any smaller, and if Abby couldn't snag a new client or two she'd be buried in them.

Her hand shook as she put on her eyeliner. "Get a hold of yourself," she muttered at her reflection. With a snap of her wrist she pulled a tissue from the box beside her, wiped off the smeared liner and put it on again. This time she managed to keep the line straight. She tossed the pencil back in its bag and stared at her brooding expression. "I can't go. I'll tell Chase—"

The doorbell rang, making her jump. She checked her watch. "Darn. He's early."

As she walked to the back door she scrambled for an excuse to get out of the party. She'd decided she would tell him she'd given herself a headache worrying about Julia, but as she stared at the man at her front door the words escaped her mind unsaid.

It wasn't the first time she had seen Chase in a suit, so she shouldn't have been surprised by how well the olive green material shaped his body— but she was. The slight frown wrinkling his forehead only made him more gorgeous.

"Abby, let me in. I'm getting soaked out here."

Saying he looked even better wet didn't seem like the appropriate response, so she stepped back and let him into the house.

It wasn't until he was inside that he really seemed to look at her. His eyes widened as he slowly took in her appearance from the top of her head to the tips of her open-toed sandals. "I don't think *beautiful* will come close to describing how you look. I'm going to have to fight off every man in the room tonight just to remain by your side."

"Thank you." His compliment made her feel pretty and feminine, even if it was too smooth to be true.

"Are you ready to go?"

"I—" She tried to recall the excuse she had planned to use.

"You're not going to back out on me, are you?" His frown was back.

"I . . . I'm not really comfortable at these things. I don't fit in." She took an involuntary step back so he wouldn't be towering over her.

"It's a Horseman's Ball. There'll be other trainers there and they'll be making contacts, which is exactly why you're going. Remember?"

"I know, I just don't—"

"If you don't go, they'll all be attacking me, trying to get me to sign on with their training programs. I would have to be polite and listen to them. What if one of them has a better selling pitch than you? I might have to change trainers."

"Oh, all right! Quit being so dramatic. I'm not quite ready yet, so you'll have to wait." She turned and darted for her bedroom, closing the door behind her.

Abby needed to stall for time. It wasn't just the party she was uncomfortable with—after all, she had faked class before when she was with Martin—it was the fact that she was going with Chase. It didn't matter that they had only shared a few kisses and nothing more; people would talk. She eyed her closet; maybe if she changed into pants she would feel less exposed to their criticism.

A soft knock sounded on her door. "Are you all right in there?"

"I'm fine. I'm . . . I'm just trying to find my . . . uh . . . shoes."

"They're on your feet!"

She looked down at the black sandals she'd been wearing when she let Chase into the house. "Oh." She was losing it.

"Are you still decent?"

"Yes."

"I'm coming in." He pushed the door open, then leaned against the frame crossing his arms. "Mind telling me what's going on?"

She flopped down on her bed and looked up at him. "I can't do this."

He shook his head. "I don't understand. Why?"

"I can't stand to be judged *yet* again. It hurt too much the last time. I've worked hard to protect myself from other people's opinions. I won't put myself out there for them to throw stones at me."

"Abby." He sat down beside her. His weight caused the bed to dip and she slid toward him until they were touching thigh to thigh. "You're not making any sense. What's this all about?"

Might as well tell him. "When I lived in Texas, I was married to man named Martin Blue. He came to the stable I worked at one day and swept me clear off my feet."

"I hope he had more finesse than you did with me," he joked.

She slapped at his arm. "Can you be serious? Martin was smart, handsome and wealthy—everything I thought I wanted in a man. I was so surprised when he asked me to marry him after only dating for two months that I never questioned why he wanted to elope. We flew to Vegas the next day and got married in the wedding chapel at our hotel."

"Vegas? You deserve better than a fly-by-night wedding. He should have known that."

Abby gave him a slight smile at his kind words. "After we came home, he took me to meet his parents. They were the most horrible people I have ever had the displeasure of associating with. They were outraged Martin would marry a *common* woman. In their opinion I had no merit as a wife because I wasn't wealthy and I had no fancy family connections they could use. It wasn't until I met them that I realized he was afraid to tell his parents about me before we were married.

"At first we both made an effort to make our marriage work and it was good. We were too busy fighting against his family and their society friends to realize how unsuited for each other we really were." She sighed, remembering the good times they had shared.

"Eventually Martin's parents wore him down and turned him against me. He tried to change me, starting with my clothes and eventually trying to get me to quit the job I loved. When I refused him he became distant. He was ashamed of me."

Chase took her hand and squeezed it, but he didn't interrupt her this time. The simple gesture was enough to give her the determination to continue.

"At the time, I was working under a trainer who was a good friend of Martin's father. With his help the Blue's were able to frame me with questionable training practices on the track. I lost my trainer's license, my job and my good reputation. When I finally proved to the Racing Commission the charges against me were false, I found I had lost my husband, as well. He preferred to be divorced from me, rather than stand up to his family any longer."

Abby finally risked a look at Chase. He was frowning

again and she had to wonder if he would judge her the same way the Blues had.

"How long were you married?"

"Three years."

"And you moved here to get away from Martin and his family?"

She nodded. "Julia came with me. It wasn't enough for them to spread lies about me. They felt they had to attack her, too. We both needed a fresh start."

"What about your family?" His mouth tightened. "Where were they when all this was happening? Did they just abandon you?"

"My two brothers, Jake and Tyler, wanted to roast Martin and his family Texas-style. I didn't want any of them to get involved. It broke my parents' hearts that I didn't come to them for help, but I didn't want them to have to pay for my mistake."

Chase turned and took her other hand in his. They had become rough after the weeks of work in the barn with her. She found she liked their callused texture better than the baby-soft palms he had when she first met him.

"You are too independent for your own good," he said. "Don't you ever lean on anyone?"

She shook her head. "It's better to depend on myself. I always know if I'm going to fall."

"I won't let you fall."

He looked into her eyes as if he was searching for the mysteries of her soul. She thought he might kiss her again, and silently hoped he would. No, it'd be a bad idea. His mind, body and soul belonged to his family and possibly still to Georgia.

But what about his heart? The question came from somewhere inside her. A voice full of hope urged her to do something crazy—like believe in him . . . trust him . . . love him. She forced herself to lean away before she gave in and threw away all caution.

Chase pulled her back in, not for a kiss, but a hug. Reluctantly she embraced him. It felt good to depend on someone, if only for a moment. He felt so solid and warm, she was sure she could stay safely in his arms forever.

"We should get going," Abby mumbled into his shoulder, not making any move to pull away.

"Are you sure you're ready?" He leaned back and looked at her.

"No, but I'm going anyway."

Chase brooded the whole way to the country club, barely speaking to Abby. How could her ex-husband have let her go so easily? Was the man blind? He should have been glad the man was out of the way, giving him a chance with her, but he wanted to kill him for hurting her so deeply. Because of Martin she'd erected walls around her heart he might never tear down.

He glanced at her and smiled when he noticed she was watching him. She smiled back and turned to look out her window. Was he any better for her than Martin had been? Was he taking her to the ball tonight so she could find more clients, or because he was trying to force her to fit into his crowd?

Chase parked as close to the entrance as he could. It was raining pretty hard by now and he wondered how they would make it into the country club without getting soaked. He hadn't remembered to bring an umbrella and Abby didn't have one either. "We could wait in the car for a few minutes."

"And have everyone wonder what we were doing to steam up the windows? No way. I'll risk getting wet, thanks." She flung open her door and made a dash for the entrance.

He had no choice but to follow. He caught up with her at the stairs. "Wait for me." They ran up together and nearly bowled over the doorman in their rush to get inside. "Sorry," he apologized.

Shaking off the rain, he was just turning around when he heard a shrill voice behind him.

"Percy-baby! There you are! I've been waiting for you."

Georgia wedged herself between him and Abby, snagging his arm. "I'm so glad you came."

"Of course I did." He tried to shake out of her grip. "The question is why are you here?" He frowned at his unsuccessful attempt to release himself. She clung to him like a burr, blocking any contact he might have with Abby.

"Oh I just couldn't wait to tell you!" she trilled. "Daddy bought me a horse. And your father was so happy about it he offered to let me use his trainer. Come with me and I'll let you meet him."

Chase heard a soft snort from the other side of Georgia. "I've already met Michael. I thought your father didn't approve of horse racing."

"He understands I just had to have one. I mean, how else am I supposed to spend time with you?"

"Georgia—"

"You spend so much time at the track," she continued over top of him.

"Georgia—"

"And when you're not there, you're at the office and I can hardly follow you there."

"Georgia!" She finally paused long enough for him to set her straight. If he didn't handle this now, Abby would never speak to him again. "We already discussed this. We're *not* involved any longer. You're not my girlfriend. Did you forget?"

She stood gaping at him with a confused expression on her face. It seemed the last thing she expected was for him to stand up to her. "But . . ."

"But nothing. We're not together and that's final."

She sunk her nails into his jacket and she pulled him down until her lips were against his ear. "I'll tell my father to pull his business," she warned.

"Go ahead." He yanked his arm from her grasp and stepped around her to get to Abby. Placing his hand at the small of her back he said, "after you."

"Mind telling me what's going on?" she asked in a lowered voice.

"Some other time." He winked at her and pushed her forward into the ballroom of the country club. "What do you think, Cinderella?"

The room was decorated with bales of straw and sheaths of wheat. An ice sculpture of a thoroughbred, his jockey astride his back, graced the center of the buffet table. Waiters swirled around the formally attired crowd with trays of appetizers and champagne.

"Wow," she whispered. "Do you know all these people?"

"Hardly." He chuckled. "I've lived in New York most of my adult life. Even my parents don't know all these people. It's the Horseman's Ball, not the Dymond's social occasion of the year."

"Right. I know that. I'm just nervous."

"Don't be. I'll be here beside you the whole time." He glanced down at her and she gave him a tremulous smile. "How about we get a drink?"

"Okay."

He took her arm and led her to the bar, stopping to talk to people along the way. He made a point of introducing her each time. There were many people by the bar and he found he had to press into her to keep her close. It wasn't an unwelcome situation. The warmth of her body drove away any remaining chill he felt from being outside. He slipped his arm around her back, pulling her a little nearer.

"What do you think you're doing?" she asked.

"Just making room for everyone else." He grinned down at Abby. She couldn't fight him without causing a scene. "What do you want?" He nudged her closer to the bar.

"I guess I'll have a red wine."

Once he got the bartender's attention he placed their order, then handed Abby's glass over a gray-haired woman's head to her waiting grasp. He took his own drink and eased out of the crowd, trying not to spill. "Ready to mingle?" he asked when he was safely away from the danger of being bumped.

"You lead, I'll follow."

Chase led her straight to Theodore Jamison who was stalking the buffet table rather than the bar. "Theo!" He waved at the portly man to get his attention. "There's someone I'd like you to meet."

"Hey, buddy. Do you have the contracts ready for me to sign yet?"

"No, but soon."

"Don't drag your feet on this. I'm serious about using your company, but I've had other offers. Right now I'm most interested in the firm that can put together the fastest campaign, not just the best one. I want to get my product on the market before someone steals my idea."

"I'll courier them over early next week."

"Good." He glanced at Abby. "This lovely lady must be Miss Blue. I hear you're the main reason for Lance's success."

"I did the training, but he has all the talent."

"I knew it!" He slapped Chase on the back. "I never should have let you have him so cheap."

"At the time he was knee-deep in mud and in bad need of a vet. I wouldn't have paid more for him than I did."

"But he had potential!"

Abby chuckled. "There are hundreds of horses out there with potential, but someone has to take the incentive to use it. Lance would still be in your field if Chase hadn't been looking to buy a horse."

"Good point. Maybe I should take a second look at my stock. There might be another gem in the barns."

Chase heard the opening he was waiting for. "You should take Abby with you. She has a great eye for horse flesh *and* she's looking to get a few more clients."

"Maybe I'll do that." He gave her a tentative smile. "If she's willing to put up with me, that is."

"Trust me, you couldn't be more trouble than any of my current clientele."

Chase chose to ignore her meaningful look. He noticed Theo was gazing at the buffet table again. "We've kept you long enough. Enjoy the ball and maybe we'll talk to you again later." He ushered Abby back into the crowd. "See . . . wasn't so bad, was it?"

"No. He seemed nice enough. Who are you going to introduce me to next?"

"How about me?" A familiar voice spoke up from beside them.

"Terry?" he asked as he took in the slender man with the shocking red hair. "What are you doing here?"

"Your father usually raffles off a few tickets at the office. This year I won one of them." He turned and stuck out his hand. "Terry Lockside, and you would be?"

"Abigail Blue." She shook hands with him, returning his smile. "But you can call me Abby."

"He can call you 'off limits'." Chase glared at them. "Easy with the charm there, buddy. She's not a party favor, she's my horse trainer."

"I can't believe it. You're far too lovely to be subjected to manual labor. I was sure you must be a princess."

Abby snorted. "I like this one. Can I take him home?"

"No. He's far less charming once you get to know him, I assure you."

She nudged Chase with her elbow. "That's not very nice."

"Ahh, but it's true, I'm afraid," Terry sighed. "My charm wears off as fast as gold plate. Lucky for me the boss here still finds me useful."

"He's the most creative man I've ever met. He could come up with an ad campaign for holey socks."

"Wow, I'm impressed. Could you convince some of these people they need me as a trainer for their horses?"

"You don't need me. I mean, I'm convinced and I don't own a horse."

Chase looked over Terry's shoulder and noticed Georgia bearing down on them, a frown marring her pristine features. "Could you excuse me a minute?" He stepped away from the group, attempting to intercept his ex-girlfriend before she caused a scene.

"I want to know what this is about, Percy!" she snapped at

him when she got close enough. "Have you lost your mind? You're embarrassing me and your family by flaunting your track trash around like she's more important to you than I am. I told you, you could have an affair, but please be a little more considerate of my feelings. People are starting to talk."

"Do I have to stand up on a table and yell it to the crowd before you'll believe me? We are not dating. With Theodore Jamison's account secured I don't need the business your father would bring to the company. As soon as Theo signs the papers, Dymond Enterprises is in the clear. And I'm warning *you* this time, Georgia, if your family tries to get any of our clients to leave the firm you'll be sued for defamation."

He ran his hand through his hair, contemplating her pinched expression. He couldn't help it, he felt guilty. "What I don't understand is why you would want to be with a man who is in love with another woman?"

"You love her?"

He was as surprised as she was. He wasn't sure when it happened, but he was in love with Abby. "Yes, I do." The words, though unfamiliar, felt right.

"I remember hearing about her when I was in Texas. She has a past, you know. Scandal follows her wherever she goes."

"If you're trying to make me think less about her, it won't work. I already know about her ex-husband and his manipulative family."

"She's not your kind," Georgia sneered. "She's blue collar and you're old money."

"I've heard enough of this." Chase was going to do something drastic if Georgia didn't stop being so rude. "You have to give me up. We're finished."

She mumbled something before whirling away from him. "What?"

She shook her head and disappeared into the crowd, but he could have sworn he heard her say, "This isn't over."

Twenty minutes later, Abby was haunting the buffet table. Terry had left her side to talk to some colleagues shortly after Chase had disappeared. She had stopped long enough to greet one of the trainers she knew, and then headed for the food. Although she knew what most of the varied appetizers were, they were far different from the simple fare she grew up on.

For a moment she felt like she was back in Martin's world. Black-tie affairs and fancy food were part of that life. She was hay and horses.

She raised her head from her perusal of the table and noticed Georgia walking toward her. This couldn't be good. She glanced around herself, but people blocked any escape she might have had from the perfect blonde.

"Miss Blue." She smiled sweetly. "I was wondering if I might have a word with you?"

"Uh . . . sure." Abby didn't think she'd cause a scene with so many people around.

"Privately."

Damn. If they were alone she could say or do anything. "How about over by the terrace?" she suggested. At least they'd still be in view of the party there.

"Splendid." Georgia hooked her arm through Abby's and led her through the crowd like they were the best of friends.

Abby wasn't fooled. The woman was playing a part for the watching crowd. She knew her game. Rule One: Only let people see what you want them to see.

They stopped by the French doors leading out to the terrace. "So, Miss Blue, Percy never formally introduced us. I'm Georgia Tiessen, Percy's girlfriend . . ." She tossed her blonde curls. "Um, ex-girlfriend. I know you train his horse. I believe he said your name is Abby?"

"Yes, it is."

"You were married to Martin Blue from Texas?"

She nodded.

"I wonder if we ever met, since we obviously traveled in the same circle. Even if it was only briefly." She smiled sweetly again.

"I doubt it. I'm sure if we had, one of us would have remembered."

"I suppose you're right. Now here we are again within the same social circle, same associates . . . same men."

"Hmm . . ." she acknowledged. Georgia was pumping her for information, hoping to find out if she shared a dirty little secret with Chase. The woman sure didn't waste any time. "I suppose."

"Of course, you're not really part of this world are you? You're just a poor working girl in a nice dress."

Abby would have been astonished, but she'd had to deal with Georgia's type in Texas. "Oh come on, Georgia, tell me how you really feel. Tell me how I'll never fit in because I have no money and no significant connections. I have to warn you, I've heard it all before."

"That's because it's true," she snarled. "You're just a conquest for Percy; a challenge he needs to overcome. He'll never fall in love with you. His family will never accept you and their opinion will, ultimately, sway his. Isn't that what happened with Martin?" The smile she gave was smug with satisfaction.

"You're mistaken if you think I'm after him as a potential husband. Our relationship is strictly business." It wasn't true. What she felt for Chase went far deeper than business. But she wouldn't admit the fact to herself, never mind someone else. "As for my marriage to Martin Blue, it's no one's concern but mine and his."

"Your little act doesn't fool me. I know you want to take my Percy from me, but it won't work. I'll get him back. And when I do I'll destroy you and your *business*. Your reputation will be as worthless as it was in Texas. I'll make sure it's so scarred you have to move to Canada to train racehorses!"

Abby fought to keep from ripping out the woman's hair. She was being very successfully baited. She had to keep her temper, or risk causing an outrageous scene and giving the blonde some much needed ammunition. "No one messes with my stable."

"We'll see." She smiled her promise before she left.

"Arghh!" She'd worked too hard to let someone like Georgia ruin her business. She'd let herself be pushed around before, but she'd had enough.

A waiter watched her nervously from the corner of the buffet table. "You're out of caviar," she said to cover her outburst.

"Oh! I'll get some more. If you'll just wait here," he nodded. "I'll be right back."

Abby had no intention of waiting for the man. If she did she'd have to eat the stuff. She'd rather chew on beach sand. Glancing around the room, she looked for a place she could escape to and calm down, but every corner was filled with people. She noted the French doors; the terrace was covered with a green and white eave. If the wind didn't pick up she'd stay dry.

She looked over her shoulder to make sure no one was watching her. Satisfied she could make a safe escape, she slipped out the door into the cool evening air. Dusk was claiming the golf course, but she could still make out the nearby greens.

It would feel wonderful to sink my feet into the lush, moist grass, she thought, wiggling her toes in her constricting sandals. She settled for resting her hands on the stone balustrade and taking a deep breath.

What could Georgia do to her? Most of her clients had been with her since she had moved to Kentucky. They weren't fabulously wealthy and they didn't give a lick about Abby's social standing. The blonde would have no influence over them.

"Would you object to my company, Miss Blue?"

Abby turned to see Percy Senior standing in the open doorway. "It's a public terrace Mr. Dymond. You can do whatever you want." She turned back to keep watch over the greens, hoping the man would go away.

"You're having a good season." He leaned a hip against the rail. "Quite a few wins actually."

"Unhappy with your trainer already?" She watched him from the corner of her eye.

"Michael gets results . . ."

"But?"

"But sometimes I wonder at his methods. I haven't seen anything, mind you. It's just a feeling I get."

"I'm not going to feed you rumors to get you to drop him, Percy. It's not my style and I have no stake in it anyway."

"You could." He looked at her.

She turned from the rail to face him. "I have my own stable to maintain."

"I understand that now and I'm willing to give you enough assistants to cover the extra work load." He returned his attention to the golf course. "What do you say, Miss Blue?"

Abby crossed her arms, perturbed by his nonchalance. "What's the catch?"

"You should know."

"Stay away from Chase." She shook her head. "Why does everyone think I'm having an affair with your son?"

"It's not so hard to imagine," he said. "He's rich and he's set to inherit the family business. You're not exactly poor, but your best friend is recovering from a career-destroying injury, and is suffering severe financial difficulties. So maybe I should ask you why you wouldn't want my son?"

No answer she could give him would come. She could hardly tell him she was afraid of making the same mistake twice, or lie to him and say she didn't desire Chase. "He's a grown man, capable of making his own decisions. You're willing to let him run the company, but won't let him choose who he wants to spend his time with. Why?"

Percy frowned at her. "Georgia is the right sort of woman for him and he loves her. He's just a little confused right now."

"Mr. Dymond, I appreciate your offer, but under the circumstances—"

"Think about it before you refuse me." He pushed away from the balustrade and left the terrace.

Abby fisted her hands on the railing and resisted the urge to scream. Of all the nerve! Bribery, threats, what else could she expect from this evening? The next rich snob to come out and talk to her could take a flying leap off the balcony for all she cared.

"There you are. I thought you left without me."

"No," she answered Chase. "But if you don't take me home now I will." He took her shoulders, but she pulled away. "Don't."

"What's going on?"

She shook her head. "I'm not feeling very well. Will you take me home?"

"As soon as you tell me what's really bothering you."

She turned to see he was standing behind her with his arms crossed. He wasn't going to give in to her feeble excuses. His belligerent stance made her temper flare higher. He was in danger of being the person to take a leap from the balcony. "Fine! If you won't drive me home I'll find my own way!"

With a quick side step she was around him. She dashed down the stone steps. From here she could get to the parking lot by cutting across the green. Once there, she could have the doorman call a cab for her.

"What the heck is going on, Abby?" He caught her arm and pulled her to a stop before she made it halfway across the green.

"Go inside, Chase." She refused to turn and look at him as she spoke. "You're getting soaked."

"No." He pulled her to face him. "Why do you want to go home?"

"Because I don't belong here. Why can't you see that? Georgia and your father had no problem pointing it out to me. This is your world, not mine."

"They said that to you?"

"Georgia did. Your father was more subtle."

He clutched her forearms, staring down at her. "I can understand Georgia going after you, but I wish my father would butt out and mind his own business."

She had calmed down enough to see the situation from Percy's perspective. "He only wants what's best for you. He's probably right. I certainly don't want to repeat my past and I'd hate to bring you down with me."

Chase didn't answer her. He just stared.

He would come to his senses now—call her a cab and make excuses for her early departure. There wasn't anything else he could do, she reasoned. It was best to make a clean break before things got too complicated.

Part of her crumbled as she realized she had hoped he would be different. *I never had a chance with him.*

Chapter Eleven

Chase urged Abby off the green and toward the parking lot. "Come on, we're going home."

"But the party . . . what will everyone think if you leave after charging out into the rain after me?"

"I don't give a damn what 'polite society' thinks." He strode angrily across the asphalt, unlocked the passenger door of his car and held it open for her.

She tried to slide in without touching him, but he grabbed her shoulders and molded her to his length.

"If their opinions hurt people . . . hurt you, then they can all go to hell." He pressed his lips hard against hers, demanding she kiss him back. She fisted her hands in his shirt, using it for balance as she raised up on her toes to gain better access to his mouth. He wanted to devour her. He needed her to understand how much he cared.

Chase tore himself away and pushed her gently down into her seat. "I have to get you home before I do something stupid." He firmly shut the door, walked to the driver's side and got in. "You might want to put on your seat belt."

She pulled the restraint across her shoulder as he wheeled out of the lot onto the road. Had it been gravel he would have left stones flying in their wake. The tension that rose between them was rich and dark like an old red wine. He longed to drink it in; swallow it in satisfying gulps. But he knew enough to savor the anticipation, enjoy the warmth spreading within as he slowly became intoxicated by the feelings surging through his heart.

Abby's farm rose up to meet them in the distance. Chase slammed the car to a halt in the driveway; gravel crunching under the tires. The rain was relentless. Water sluiced down over the windshield, making it hard to see the back door to her house.

Chase sighed loudly and dropped his head onto the steering wheel. "I can't do this."

"It's because of me isn't it? You've finally realized I'm not good enough for you." She grabbed the door handle. "It's okay . . . I understand."

"Let me explain."

Abby shook her head and dove out of the car into the pouring rain. She fished her key out of her purse as she ran up the front steps. She struggled to find the lock through the blanket of rain.

"I . . . can't . . . open . . . the . . . door!" She twisted the handle and turned into his arms at the same time, half-walking, half-falling through the doorway. The screen slammed shut behind them, but neither of them bothered to close the door.

"Chase, go home. I don't want you to stay out of pity for me."

"I'm not going anywhere until you let me finish what I was saying. And for the record, I have never pitied you." He tightened his grip on her to keep her from running away again.

"I don't think I want to hear this."

"I think you do." He stared down at her as he talked. "I can't have a one-night stand with you, Abby. You mean more to me than that. And I respect you too much to get involved while I'm still trying to resolve things with Georgia. When we're together I want it to be forever."

A deep rumble of thunder shook the house and the wind threw the rain against the screen door. Was the weather an omen? Did the storm represent the turmoil they would face if they ever got together?

"Do you think we have a chance at forever, Chase?"

He let her go, shut the front door and leaned against it. "I don't know, but I want to try and I'm not leaving until you give me that chance." Another crack of thunder rattled the house.

"I don't think you should go anywhere tonight. It's not safe to drive in this weather. I've got some extra bedding in the hall closet. You can sleep on the couch."

He followed her down the hall. "You haven't answered my question. Will you at least accept the fact that there is something more than great chemistry between us?"

"I know there is, Chase," she said as she pulled sheets from the closet and thrust them at his chest. "And I want to explore what we have, too."

Abby awoke to bright sunlight streaming through her bedroom window. She stretched, enjoying the warmth it sent through her. She'd slept in and didn't care. Life was just too good to care about the little things.

"Are you getting up this morning, or are you going to sleep the whole day away?" She heard Chase call from the other room.

"Coming!" She slipped out of bed and hurried to put on some clothes. Stopping by the bathroom on her way to the kitchen, she took care of necessities and washed up. A shower would have to wait until later.

As she came into the kitchen she was greeted with a steaming hot cup of coffee and a brief kiss on the lips from Chase. "Morning," she murmured as he pulled away.

"Morning." He guided her to one of the bar stools with his hand on her back. "How do you like your eggs?"

"Over—" The ringing of the phone interrupted her. She hopped off the stool and grabbed the receiver off the wall.

"Hello?"

"Abby!" Mel practically yelled into the phone. "Thank goodness you're home. You've got to get to the track now. We've got major problems."

"Oh no!" She glanced at Chase. "Is one of the horses hurt?" He put down the frying pan he was holding and focused his attention on her.

"The horses are fine, but Doc Casey's here with one of the track officials. They're searching the tack stall."

She frowned. Why would they want to go through her stuff? She didn't use anything on her horses that could be considered a banned substance. "Let them look. They won't find anything."

"Boss . . . they found syringes."

"What?! I'll be there as fast as I can, Mel. Don't let them leave before I get there." She'd barely had the phone hung up before she was running for the door.

"Abby, slow down." Chase grabbed her arm.

"I've got to go," she said, pulling from his grasp. "I'll explain later."

"You're really upset. Let me drive you."

"No. I'll be fine. I can handle this myself. Someone's trying to get my license suspended, but I'll be damned if I let it happen to me again."

"What?" He moved to block the door.

"Someone must have told the track officials they suspected I was drugging my horses. They searched my tack stall this morning and found syringes."

"Are they yours?"

It was a reasonable question, but Abby took offence to it anyway. She needed Chase to stand by her right now, not question her ethics. "I do *not* needle my horses," she ground out between clenched teeth.

"I didn't mean—"

She pushed past him and strode out the door. She didn't have time for his apology and she wasn't interested in it. "Do me a favor and lock the door before you leave." She dashed down the back steps and jumped into her truck.

By the time she reached the back entrance to the track she had decided on two things. The first was that she had been way too hard on Chase and he deserved an apology. He had asked an innocent question and she had snapped at him.

The second was that she couldn't afford to lose her license—even temporarily. Julia, Mel and Jim were counting on her for their livelihoods. She wouldn't be the only one suffering a loss of income.

Abby parked in the designated lot and walked to her barns with a purpose. This time no one was going to push her away from the job she loved. She heard Mel's raised voice before she saw her.

As she rounded the corner the scene unfolded. Mel was shouting at Doc Casey and the steward while Jim held her back by her shoulders. "Easy, Melanie," Abby said, once she was close enough to be heard. "Yelling isn't going to solve anything."

"Miss Blue." The track vet nodded his acknowledgment.

He wasn't the friendliest person on a good day. Today his demeanor was as cool as a northern wind. "Morning, gentlemen." Abby took on a business tone. "I've been told we have a problem here, but I'm sure it's just a misunderstanding."

"No misunderstanding, Miss Blue. I got an anonymous phone call this morning. The caller said she saw you giving one of your horses a shot and she was concerned for its safety." He shook a plastic bag filled with syringes at her. "We found drug paraphernalia in your tack stall this morning."

"Be reasonable, Doctor Casey. None of my horses have tested positive for drugging."

"There are substances we can't test for yet and new ones coming onto the market all the time."

"And did you find any of those drugs in my barns?"

"No, but you know as well as I do that just possessing the syringes is cause for immediate suspension."

"You can't do this!" She took a deep breath and quieted her voice. "Those aren't mine."

"Then perhaps you can tell us who they belong to?"

"No, I can't. Someone planted those in my tack stall."

"That's not a good enough answer, Miss Blue," the steward said. "Your license is suspended until further notice." Both men brushed silently past her without even a good-bye.

She was numb inside and out. This wasn't supposed to happen, not again. She was supposed to save the day. She was Superwoman, that's what she did. If she couldn't help the people she loved then she was worthless.

Chapter Twelve

Chase didn't know what to do. He wanted to wait at Abby's until she got back, but he didn't want to see her. He was angry at her for taking her problems out on him, and at the same time he wanted to take her into his arms and protect her from anymore hurt.

He had to do something, so he drove home. He needed a shower and something to eat before he'd be able to think straight. Then he was going to confront Georgia and see if she had anything to do with the mysterious syringes. Once he cleared up this mess Abby would have to know how serious he was about her.

The house was quiet when he slipped through the front door. He was glad no one was there waiting to ambush him and question where he had been the night before. He even managed to avoid Roger as he crept up the stairs and opened the door to his room.

He put fresh clothes on the bathroom counter and turned on the shower before undressing. Warm steam surrounded him when he opened the shower door and stepped in. The spray refreshed his body, but did little to settle his mind.

Abby's problem wouldn't wash away as easily as soap on

skin. After he found out who left the syringes he would have to approach the racing committee and convince them she was innocent. He hoped if they had pulled her license already they would reinstate it as quickly.

He knew how important her job and her reputation were to her. If she lost the ability to support herself and her employees, she would lose her independence. She would consider herself a failure, whether she was or not.

Chase turned off the shower and stepped out. After he toweled off and dressed he went to the mirror. A quick shave and he would be done. When he was finished, he wiped off a few smears of shaving cream with a damp washcloth, then headed downstairs to the kitchen and the smell of frying bacon. His stomach rumbled as he pushed open the door, reminding him he hadn't eaten much the night before.

Roger set a plate down in front of him without asking if he wanted breakfast. He dug into the food before the butler returned with his own plate and sat down across from him.

"Are you going into the office today?"

"I'm not sure . . . but that reminds me, I have to have Margaret courier over Theo's contract this morning." He pushed himself away from the table and went over to the phone. She picked up on the second ring.

"Good morning, Dymond Enterprises, how may I help you?"

"Morning, Margaret. I need a favor." He checked the clock on the wall. Theo probably wouldn't be out of bed yet. "Can you have the Swiss Chip contract couriered over to Theo's home address sometime before lunch?"

"Yes, sir. Is there anything else?"

Chase heard a suspicious click and cracked open the kitchen door enough to see Georgia replacing the receiver on the hall phone by the library. Had she been listening to his call? Maybe she thought he was talking to Abby and hung up when she realized it was just business.

"No, that's it. Thanks, Margaret." He hung up the phone

and swung open the door the rest of the way before Georgia could escape. Her gaze snapped up to meet his as he strode down the hall.

"Morning Percy-darling, did you enjoy the ball last night?"

"Most of it." He took her elbow and ushered her into the library. "Can we talk for a minute?"

"I think you said enough last night," she said as they cleared the doorway. She ripped her arm from his grasp. "What else could you possibly have to say to me?"

There was no good way to charge your ex-girlfriend with framing your current girlfriend. Chase tried to think of a delicate way to broach the subject, but in the end he gave up and asked her. "Where did you get the syringes, Georgia?"

"Whatever are you talking about?"

"And while I'm asking, how did you smuggle them into Abby's tack stall?" He crossed his arms and glared at her. No way would he fall for her *innocent* act. He knew better.

"Just what sort of absurd crime are you accusing me of, Percy?" She put her hands on her hips. Her manicured red nails cut into her white skirt.

"Abby got a phone call this morning that the track officials found syringes in her tack stall. All forms of drug paraphernalia are illegal in the backstretch."

"Well, that's hardly my problem," she huffed.

"Someone tipped them off, and someone planted those syringes."

"You don't think they're hers, even though she's been accused of drugging her horses before?" The smile she gave him was a smug one.

"She was framed then, too, but I suspect you already knew about it."

"Hmm . . . could be, I never heard otherwise. I can tell you the Blues were well respected within their social circle and if they kicked your little trainer out of their family then she clearly wasn't up to their standards."

"They're snobs, but they aren't the issue right now, are they?

I want to know if you planted those syringes." Chase was losing patience with her petty comments and tiring games.

"Or else what? You have nothing left to throw at me and you know it."

"Really?" He raised an eyebrow. "I can think of at least one reason for you to answer my question. Do you want everyone in Kentucky and in our personal circle of friends to know I dumped you? For a poor, working girl? There are tabloids out there that eat this sort of thing up. They'll make Abby look like Cinderella and you'll be one of the wicked step-sisters."

She cast her hands down from her waist, balling them into fists. Her skin deepened into an unattractive shade of red. "You wouldn't!"

"I'm not asking for much Georgia, just the truth."

"So what if I did frame her!" She stomped her foot on the floor. "It was beyond easy and she deserves it. That tramp stole you away from me."

"You never had me."

"Yes, I did. You were mine. We would still be together if it weren't for her. For all I know I could have been planning my own wedding by now. I'd finally be free of my family and that stupid 'Tidy Toilet Bowl Princess' title. If I'm going to suffer, so is she."

"No." He took her by the shoulders. "You've got two choices, Georgia. You can refuse to clear Abby's name and I'll call the tabloids and tell them the Tidy Toilet Bowl Princess has been flushed. Or you can come to the racetrack with me and explain to the track officials what you did, how you did it, and why you did it. In exchange for your cooperation I'll cover up your involvement in this scandal and your reputation will remain unscathed. Which one is it going to be?"

"Fine, Chase. I'll go with you. I'll tell them everything. But one day you'll realize she's not good enough for you and you won't have me to come back to. You'll regret this."

* * *

Abby couldn't breathe. Her world was tumbling down around her and she was suffocating. She wanted to be with Chase. He would wrap her in his arms and kiss her troubles away, at least for a little while. But when she got home he was already gone. Instead of facing her problems in her lonely house, she jumped back in her truck and went to see Julia. As her business partner, she deserved to know what was going on.

Julia was laying on the couch with her leg up on a stack of pillows when Abby walked into her living room. "What's wrong?"

Abby glanced at Rob, who had followed her in from the doorway. She bit her lip and tried to think of a way to soften the news. There was way no way around it. The two of them had been depending on her and she had failed. Again. "I got a phone call to go to the track this morning. They suspended my trainer's license."

"What?" Julia struggled to sit up until her husband walked around to the back of the couch and helped her. "They can't do that. What reason could they possibly have for suspending you?"

Abby dropped onto the plush footstool at the end of the couch. She pushed her hands through her hair, then dropped them into her lap. "Someone called the track officials in to check the tack stall for drugs. Doc Casey found syringes. He suspended me on the spot. I had to have Jim and Mel pack up the horses and our equipment because they wanted me to leave the backstretch immediately." She felt a tear slip down her cheek and hung her head in humiliation. How could she have let this happen?

"It's the damn Blue family! Can't they leave you alone? I'm going to Texas and I'm going to strangle them all with my bare hands!"

"Easy, honey, you're not going anywhere in your condition. Let Abby finish."

Abby raised her head and looked at the couple watching her. Rob stood behind Julia caressing her shoulders. Just once she wished she could depend on someone like that. "I don't think it's Martin's family. I haven't had any contact with them since the divorce became final."

"Then who? Who would be so vindictive?"

"I don't want to think of the possibilities. We've been doing well with our horses this year. It could be anyone from a jealous business acquaintance to someone with a more personal agenda." It wasn't hard to point a finger with people like Georgia and Percy Sr. plotting against her.

"Do you think it's someone who knows about your past?"

"I wouldn't be surprised. It's too similar to what happened before."

"But we had locks on the doors. How did they get in?"

"They're standard locks. It wouldn't be hard to find a duplicate key."

"We're getting better ones as soon as you're reinstated."

"The horse is already out of the barn, Julia." She hated to bring up what she was about to say, but it was necessary. "We're ignoring the bigger problem. With my license suspended and you in rehabilitation, there's no one to race the horses. How long before we start to lose clients? How long before—" She gulped in some air and tried to regain control over her emotions. "I'm sorry, you guys. I promised to take care of you and help you out. I'm such a failure." The final sentence came out as a whisper, and she dropped her head into her hands.

"No, you're not!"

Rob came up behind her and pulled her into a hug. "We never expected you to support us." He pushed her over to Julia's waiting embrace.

She kneeled by her friend and accepted the awkward hug.

"Abby, we're going to be okay. You just worry about yourself."

"But what about the house payments, and your hospital bills and Rob's job?" She glanced between the two of them, noting their exchanged shrug.

"I was waiting for the right time to tell you and now definitely isn't it, but you deserve to know . . ."

"What?"

"We're selling the house—"

"No! Where will you live?"

"Let me finish. Mr. Dymond has offered the apartment above his barns to us, free of charge."

"But he saves that for his head trainer."

"I know."

The revelation burned as it sunk in. "You're dropping me for Percy Dymond?"

"I'm not dropping you. You're still my friend and business partner. You wanted me to change jobs. I thought you'd be glad I found something I liked."

"You could have trained with me. You still can. I can get more clients . . ."

Julia shook her head. "I don't think that's such a good idea. If I spread out my investments, then I won't have to worry if one of them falls through. I'll train for Percy and remain your silent partner. Then if you ever need my help—"

Abby stood up. "You really think Mr. Dymond will be happy to find out you're still partners with me after you start working for him?"

"I've already discussed it with him. He's not pleased, but he accepted my terms. Don't you see he's trying to compensate me for the fall? He feels really guilty about it. He wants to fire Michael, but he has to wait until I'm recovered enough to take over. Please don't be mad."

"I understand why you feel you have to do this." She turned to leave. "But I can't deal with it right now. I'll talk to you when I cool off." She was in such a hurry to leave, she almost ran out the door.

Jim and Mel were unloading horses when Abby pulled into the driveway. She sat in her truck, staring at the Shady Blue Stables sign on the side of the trailer. She should have known keeping her ex-husband's last name, and using it in her stable name, was bad luck. Martin would be doing the happy-jig-of-joy over her misfortune if he knew.

"How are you holding up, boss?" Mel asked when she finally got out of her truck.

"As good as can be expected, I guess. At least I'm not hiding under the bed crying my eyes out."

Jim clamped an arm around her shoulders and gave her a little squeeze. "I'm not sure things will ever get bad enough for you to lay down and give up."

She smiled tightly up at him. "I appreciate your confidence in me, but if you can't find me in the morning you know where to look."

He dropped his arm. "It's going to be all right, Abby. You'll see."

Chase's little black car pulled up beside her truck. He jumped out, carrying a bottle of champagne and bouquet of flowers. "I've got great news!"

"Well spit it out, Mr. Dymond. We could use some good news right now," Mel said.

"Abby might want to check her answering machine first."

"Huh?"

"Don't ask questions, just do it."

She shrugged her shoulders at her employees and ran into the kitchen. The machine had two messages on it. She hit rewind. The first one was from her brother Jake. After the beep the second message began to play. "Miss Blue, this is Neil Harris from the racing commission. We're pleased to tell you that after re-evaluating your case we are reinstating your license, effective immediately. Your license will be at the security shack the next time you check in. If you have any questions, you may contact me by phone or drop by my office."

She let out a whoop and burst out the door to her waiting friends. "I got my license back!" she said from the back porch. She glanced at Chase. "You did this?"

He nodded.

She leapt down the stairs into his waiting arms. "Thank you, thank you, thank you!" The kiss she gave him was enthusiastic and loud. "But how did you do it?"

He let her go and regarded her cautiously. "I had my suspicions it was Georgia who called in the complaint about you. When I confronted her about it she admitted she had bribed Michael Dover to plant the syringes in your tack stall. I was able to convince her to go to the racing commission and tell them what she had done. Considering the new evidence, the track officials felt obliged to reinstate your license. Georgia and Michael have both been suspended from the track indefinitely."

Abby didn't know what to say. Chase had gone out of his way to set things right for her. After so many years of standing up for herself it felt strange to have someone else take care of her. She was in his debt. "How can I ever repay you?"

"I don't expect payment. I did it because it was the right thing to do and because I care," he looked down at the ground, then back at her, before adding, "about you."

Mel chose that moment to break in. "So is the champagne for all of us?"

"Brat," Jim said. "You have all the subtlety of a tap dancing elephant."

"It's okay." Chase held the bottle up to the group. "I brought it for everybody." He handed the flowers to Abby. "I brought these for you."

She smiled. "Thanks. I'll put them in some water and try to find some glasses."

As luck would have it, she still had all her china from her first marriage. None of it was particularly old or valuable so she didn't worry much over bringing the four champagne flutes out to the barnyard.

She left the house to see Chase barely miss Jim's head as he popped the cork on the bottle. "Hey, I can't afford to have another employee off for an injury. Who would carry the heavy stuff if Jim was laid up?"

"Glad to know you still need me, boss. Really."

"Don't mention it." She handed around the glasses, holding Chase's while he poured.

They toasted to the happy ending of a bad day. After they had drunk their champagne and reloaded the horses, Jim and Mel left.

Chase set their glasses on the ground and took her into his arms. Her hair stirred as he placed light kisses on her forehead. "You never let anyone take care of you. I'm glad I could help you today."

She pulled away enough so she could look in his eyes. "How did you do it? How did you convince Georgia to admit to the racing commission she framed me?"

"Well . . ." Chase released her from his embrace. "First I had to goad her into admitting her guilt. Once she did, I decided to use her vanity and her ego against her." He picked up the glasses and the bottle and began walking toward the house.

Abby followed.

"So I told her if she talked to the racetrack officials I would cover up her involvement in this incident. It would kill her to have the tabloids find out how low she would go to keep a man. It was a simple solution and I managed to solve two problems with one move. Oh that reminds me, can you tell Jim and Melanie not to mention Georgia's participation in your suspension?"

All the warm feelings Abby had been feeling turned cold and prickly. Chase was protecting Georgia by keeping quiet about her stunt and by letting her sneak away. Martin's words taunted her. *Be a good girl, Abby. There's no sense getting your feathers ruffled. This is the way things are done, but if you keep your mouth shut everything will turn out fine in the end.* Her ex-husband had, of course, meant fine for him. She was cast out of his life in disgrace.

Chase put the glasses in the sink. "How about I take you out to dinner and we can celebrate?" He opened the cupboard door at his feet and placed the bottle in the small box there.

"You have to be kidding me!" She would not let Georgia continue to manipulate both their lives. "Why are you protecting her? What are you going to do for her next? Marry her so she won't be embarrassed you dumped her?"

"No! Don't be silly. Georgia and I have an agreement." He took her shoulders in his hands. "I love you, nothing she does will change the way I feel. I did this for you."

"You have a strange way of showing your love, Chase." Her voice vibrated with emotion. "I thought you were different, but you can't even stand up for me when I need you to." She pushed his hands off her shoulders.

He plunged his hands into his hair, letting them fall uselessly to his sides. "I promised her, Abby. I won't back out of the deal now, it wouldn't be right."

"Of course it wouldn't and you always do what's proper, don't you?" She crossed her arms. "Except where I'm concerned. How does Mummy and Dear Old Dad feel about me? They must be appalled you're spending time with a lowly piece of track trash."

"Why are you so mad? I was only trying to help you. Is that your problem? You can't stand having someone take care of you for a change?"

Her body stiffened in response to his question. Did she have a problem? Did letting Chase help her make her weak? She refused to believe he was right. "You just don't get it."

"Maybe I do. Maybe you're the one who doesn't understand."

"I want you to leave. Get out."

"I'll leave the house, Abby." He flung open the screen door. "But you won't kick me out of your life as easily."

Chapter Thirteen

Abby dragged herself into the house after her exhausting day at the track. The effort to drive Chase from her head brought her nothing but sore muscles and a tired body.

She left her shoes at the door. Opening the fridge, she stared inside unseeingly. She really should eat something. The light went off as she closed the door. She had no appetite.

The phone rang and she snatched up the receiver, hoping and dreading it would be Chase. "Hello?"

"Hey, Ab-a-bale! It's your most favorite brother."

Abby smiled despite her mood. She hadn't spoken to Tyler in months. It was good to hear his voice. "Hey, Toddler. Who says you're my favorite?"

"Well, I'm the handsomest, most charming, smartest sibling, so naturally I must be your favorite . . . and everyone else's, of course."

"Okay, sure. Which bridge are you trying to sell me today?"

A short bark of laughter sounded at the other end of the line. "No bridge, but I wanted to know if you would go in on a gift with me for Jake and Marni's baby?"

"What did you have in mind?"

"How about a stroller? One of the ones with the thick

wheels, cause you know Marni's going to haul that kid everywhere. They'll probably have to replace the tires before the baby's first birthday."

"Considering Jake and Marni's love of the rodeo, their kid is going to see more miles than my pickup truck. The stroller's a good idea. Do you want me to get it? I can bring it down to the ranch when I go for a visit next month."

"Sure, I'll send you some money."

Abby bit her lip before asking her question. She didn't talk about her personal life with her family, but she needed advice and she wasn't ready to talk to Julia yet. "Tyler . . . am I too controlling? What I mean is, do I push people away in order to do things myself."

"Uh . . . well . . . sometimes, yeah. You always wanted to do your own thing when we were kids, but since your divorce it's like you don't trust anyone to help you out. Not even your own family."

She clenched her fist around the phone cord. Had she pushed Chase away because of his loyalty to his family, or because he got her trainer's license back and she didn't want to be indebted to him?

"What's this all about?"

Something between a sob and a laugh left her throat. "A guy, what else?"

"Listen, Abby, I don't know the situation, but you've got to learn to trust again. You've got to get on with your life. Don't let one failure stop you from trying again."

"Fine advice from you, brother. Have you even had a relationship since Cassie ran out on your wedding day?"

"No, not really. It's hard to do when I'm always hopping from ship to ship."

"Excuses—"

"I know. That's why I'm quitting the cruise line. I haven't told the rest of the family, so don't mention it, but I have one more two-week cruise to do, then I'm leaving. I'm going to find a small town that needs a doctor and set up a practice.

Maybe if I'm lucky I'll find a small town girl to settle down with."

"Whoa! I had no idea you were so unhappy on the ship."

"Not unhappy, just lonely."

The statement resonated deep within her. She had been content before she met Chase, but deep down she longed for somebody to share her life with. She'd never admit her secret wish out loud, but it didn't stop the ache. "Yeah, I get that."

"I know you do. Of all the ways you could aspire to be like me, sis, this isn't one of them."

"I have no desire to be like you, Ty."

"But, why not?" She heard the smile in his voice. "I'm great in so many ways."

"You must have to beat the women off with your tongue depressors, doc."

"Don't I wish. I've got to go, Abby. Take it easy and listen to your big-little brother for once. Don't push this guy away just because he butts into your life once in a while. He's just trying to show you he cares."

"Okay, Ty, maybe I will. Love you."

"Me too, sis." A soft click ended the conversation.

She hung up the phone, but it rang again before she could walk away from it. She glanced at the number. It was Chase. "I'm not ready to talk to you yet. I want you to take your horse home," she said into the receiver when she lifted it to her lips.

"I'm not taking Lance home, and we have to talk about this. You've been avoiding me for three days. I have a wedding to go to in three weeks and I want you to be my date. Talk to me, Abby."

She leaned against the wall and sighed. "Are you going to keep protecting Georgia?"

"If you would just realize I'm doing this for you."

"You're not doing it for me. You're doing it to save face . . . your family's, Georgia's and your own. Don't make yourself out to be a hero. It's not like you're making a great sacrifice for me."

"You have no idea what kind of sacrifices I've made for the people I love."

"You're right, Chase. I have no idea what kind of man you are. You accuse me of keeping you out of my life, but you haven't let me into yours either. I'm starting to get the feeling you're ashamed of me."

"That's not true."

"You think I'm shutting you out, but I'm only trying to protect myself. Give me a reason to believe in you and I'll give you another chance."

"Abby, I want you to meet my friends so I can prove to you that I'm not ashamed to be with you. I'm not like your ex-husband. But I'm not backing out of the arrangement I made with Georgia. I gave her my word."

"That's what I thought." She set the receiver down.

She walked to her room and sank down on the bed. The ceiling fan whirled in a lazy circle above her head. Dust motes played in the sunlight coming through the parted curtains. It was a beautiful afternoon, but inside it felt like rain. Letting Chase go would be easier if she didn't already love him so much.

"Damn!" Chase finally slammed down the receiver on the dead phone line. He clenched the edge of the table, his thoughts turned inward. He felt the overwhelming need to take action, but he didn't know what to do.

In a burst of inspiration he pulled out the phone book, rifled through the pages until he found what he was looking for, and dialed the number.

"Hello?" A female voice responded after the first ring.

"Julia it's—"

"Chase? Why are you calling me? Is something wrong? Is it Abby?"

"She won't talk to me. I need your help."

"I can't help you." Her sigh echoed across the phone line. "She won't talk to me either."

He shook his head in confusion. "She won't? Why?"

"Long story . . . mostly she's mad because I took a job with your father. Why is she giving you the silent treatment?"

"Well . . ." He struggled with his answer, but managed to tell her what had happened between him and Abby.

"Jeez, Chase, even if she was speaking to me what could I do? You've dug your own grave."

"Julia . . . I brought Georgia to Balesworth to save my family's company. Everyone thinks we were serious and soon to be engaged, because she convinced them it was the truth. Georgia promised to bring some much needed business to Dymond Enterprises if I played by her rules. I've since taken care of the problems in the company but I felt like I owed it to her to do this one last thing so she could preserve her dignity."

"Good glory, you're as bad as Abby. If you weren't trying to solve your parents' problems—"

"I wouldn't have met Abby. Please, Julia, just try to talk to her. If she won't come around, then try to get her to the church two weeks from Saturday. I'm in a friend's wedding party that day and I wanted her to be my date. I'll prove to her and everyone there that I love her."

On the Saturday morning of Al's wedding, at five minutes to eleven, Chase walked out of the minister's office, stood in front of the altar and prayed Abby would show up. He turned to look out over the congregation. It had been a week since his last conversation with Julia and she still couldn't get Abby to talk to her.

He patted down the left lapel of his jacket, feeling for the two ring boxes. One held the wedding bands for Al and his bride the other had an engagement ring inside. His fingers clenched around the two lumps and he forced them to relax. He dropped his arm back down to his side.

"I'm supposed to be the nervous one, buddy." Al clenched his shoulder and released it. Chase and Al had been best friends since junior high, but during the past few months they had hardly seen each other. Between Al's wedding plans and Chase's new job, there just hadn't been much time for socializing.

"It will all be over soon," he whispered to his friend. "For better or for worse," he added with a chuckle. The comment earned him a jab and a wink from one of the five other groomsmen. They seemed more like a parade than a wedding party.

When the organ music started up he nearly jumped out of his shoes. He glanced down the aisle only to discover to his horror that Georgia was sashaying down the aisle to find a seat on the groom's side. She was swathed in yards of pink satin, with a train trailing behind her that would rival the bride's.

"Holy hell." He whispered to himself. "What is *she* doing here?"

Al gave him a startled look, but was distracted from commenting as the bridesmaids began their procession down the aisle. Each one was dressed in a different color of the rainbow, kind of like the sprinkles on an ice cream cone.

Chase dared another look at Georgia and she gave him a little wave and a saccharine smile. He noticed her parents had accompanied her to the ceremony, though he couldn't fathom why. Maybe she brought them as backup, because she had to know he was going to put up a fight. Rudy Tiessen glared at him and Glory practically snarled. Georgia must have told them about the break up.

He glanced around the rest of the church, but there was no sign of Abby. One battle at a time, he reminded himself. As the organist switched over to the bride's entrance hymn, he brought his focus back to the task at hand. First the wedding, then Georgia, then kissing Abby back to her senses . . . yeah, that sounded like a plan.

Al's fiancée, Laurel, glided up the aisle on her father's arm.

Al took a few steps forward to meet them. Her father shook his hand and gave his daughter a kiss on the cheek before turning to find his seat on the first pew.

The couple took the last few steps to the altar together. Happiness shone on their faces as they nodded to the minister to begin. The ceremony was going smoothly, until the minister asked if there were any objections.

"I have an objection!" Georgia's father boomed while a horrified congregation turned in their seats to stare at him.

"Daddy, no!" Georgia gave a futile tug on his arm that did little more than annoy him further.

"I object to this smug, two-timing, worthless, horse's behind making a mockery of my daughter."

The minister cleared his throat and glanced at Al. "You mean the groom's been cheating on his fiancée?"

"No! I'm talking about the best man." A collective sigh ran through the church.

"Sir, the objection is supposed to be in regards to the couple getting married."

"I don't give a rat's—"

"Mr. Tiessen, I don't think this is the time or place for this conversation," Chase reasoned. He gave Al and Laurel an apologetic shrug, but they seemed more fascinated by the proceedings than they were mad. Well . . . at least they would have a wedding to remember.

"I really don't care what you think." Rudy pushed his way out of the pew. "For some unknown reason, my daughter wants to be with you—and what my baby girl wants, my baby girl gets." He stood in the aisle with his hands on his hips.

"Not this time, I'm afraid," Chase said. "I'm in love with someone else."

His father jumped up from his pew. "It's that Blue woman, isn't it?"

"Yes, Dad. It's Abby."

His mother stood up and took her husband's hand. "Are you sure about this Blue woman? I mean, are you sure Abigail is the right woman for you?

"Yeah." He smiled briefly, nodding to himself. "Positive."

"If she makes you happy, Percy . . ."

"She does!"

"Then I think she'll make a fine addition to our family."

"Daddy!" Georgia wailed, no longer content to be ignored.

"Now wait just one damn minute!" Mr. Tiessen bore down on Chase and grabbed him by his jacket lapels. His bulk made up for his lack of height, as he easily pulled him down until they were nose to nose. "Do you mean you're abandoning my little girl for another woman? I won't stand for it. I'll sue."

"Now Mr. Tiessen . . . sir . . ." Chase pulled himself free. "Would you really want your daughter to be with a man who doesn't love her? Who could never make her happy?" Rudy didn't look convinced. "I don't think she loves me either, sir."

"Of course she does! Why else would she want a loser like you?"

"Why don't you ask her?"

Abby glanced at her watch while she wheeled around another corner. *Eleven o'clock. Damn, I'm never going to make it on time.* She was still ten miles away from church and the service was already starting.

Julia had found her in the barn this morning, cleaning out the stalls. She had come prepared for a battle. "What are you doing here?"

"What does it look like I'm doing?" Abby was surly from her sleepless night. She didn't need her best friend's help to feel worse.

"That's not what I meant and you know it. Chase is expecting you at that church and you're not there."

"What does it matter if I'm there or not? It doesn't change anything." She picked at the wooden handle of the pitchfork she was holding.

"So you're just giving up?" Julia shifted her weight on her crutches. "You're going to let Georgia win?"

Abby's head snapped up. "What do you mean?"

"She's fought pretty hard to get Chase. Do you really think she's just going to let you have him now?"

"But—"

"But? But you're a fool who won't take a chance on the best thing that has every strolled into this barn? But you're too stubborn to let Chase into your life when he clearly makes you happier than you've ever been?"

"It's more than what you said. It's the fact that I can never be more than second best in his life. He'll always choose his family over me."

"Do you know why he brought Georgia to Kentucky with him?"

"No, why?"

"He was trying to save his family's business. She offered him a way to save it, in exchange for his cooperation. He was going to sacrifice his whole life for his parents."

"You're only proving my point, Jules."

"No. You're hearing, but you're not listening. He was willing to give up his happiness because he loves his family. Think what he'd do for the woman he loves."

"He'd do anything for me," Abby sniffed. "Just like I'd do for him."

"Have you told him that?"

"No."

"Then go to the church and tell him how you feel before Georgia figures out a way to take him from you. This guy's worth fighting for, Abby. Trust me."

"You're right. She tossed the pitchfork into the wheelbarrow. Can you call Mel to finish up the barn chores?"

"I'll get Rob to do it. He's waiting for me in the car. You really didn't think I drove over here myself, did you?"

She gave Julia a quick hug. "I didn't think at all."

And she didn't think she would make it on time. She shouldn't have taken the time to clean up and put on the sundress she was wearing. She slammed on her brakes in front of the church, barely stopping before she hit the flower-covered limo. The doors to the inner sanctum banged against the wall as she ran inside. She blurted out an "I'm sorry," before she took in the scene.

The minister stood at the front of the church with the bridal party, Georgia, a heavy-set man with blond hair and Chase. She paused halfway up the aisle to stare at him. He was gorgeous in his tuxedo. It made her self-conscious and she almost ran back out of the church. How could she expect a man as perfect as him to love a country mouse like her?

Because I love him, she reminded herself. And in her heart she knew he felt the same way about her.

He took a step toward her before Georgia pushed him aside.

"You!" She screeched as she marched down the aisle. "You've ruined everything. Now I'll have to be the Tidy Toilet Bowl Princess forever!" She charged at Abby with her right arm drawn back for a swing.

She managed to duck under the wild punch, but stepped on the short train of Georgia's pink satin dress in the process. Her foot slid on the slippery material. Chase jumped to her rescue, but also began to slide on the shiny fabric.

They tumbled to the floor. Abby gasped as he hit his head on one of the pews. His eyes rolled back before his lids closed over them. "Chase!" She cradled his face in her hands. "Chase, don't do this to me."

"Is he all right?"

She looked up into the many concerned faces hovering over them, including the bride and groom. "I don't know. He won't wake up."

"Somebody get him some ice."

"Doesn't anyone care about me?" Georgia's whine carried over the crowd.

"I care." A redhead with a sequined violet dress on, wearing a scowl to match, appeared beside Abby. "I care that my daughter is a spoiled brat who would force a man to be with her because she is embarrassed of what her family does for a living. Well, guess what? If you're so ashamed of me and your father, then you can move out and find a job of your own."

"But, Mommy!" Georgia followed the angry redhead out of the church. I didn't say I was embarrassed . . ." Her voice faded away as they left the sanctuary.

The heavy-set, blond man with the moustache stopped beside Percy Sr. "I'll be taking my business elsewhere, Dymond." He looked down at Abby and grunted. "I wouldn't wish this crazy family on anyone. Good luck, you're going to need it." With a short huff, he left the church.

"Here's the ice, dear." Sara Dymond knelt on the other side of her son.

Abby took it and moved so she could rest Chase's head on her lap. "Wake up, please," she pleaded with him. She put the ice on his temple. A lump was already beginning to form. His eyes fluttered open and she fell into their gray depths. "Hi, Sleeping Beauty," she sighed with relief.

"Hi, Cinderella." He smiled. "Haven't we been here before?"

"Something like this." She brushed his hair back from his face.

"Something like this . . . but completely different. I hope you won't send me back to my girlfriend this time."

"Not unless I'm her."

"I think I can do you one better." He tried to sit up, but groaned and dropped his head back into her lap. "Could you reach into my left breast pocket and pull out the boxes?"

She put the ice pack down and stretched across his chest. Her hand shook as she slipped it inside his jacket to find two felt containers. She pulled them out.

Chase took the gray one from her and put it back in his pocket, before taking the dark blue one and opening it. A horseshoe decorated with small diamonds sat on a thin gold band. "I realize it's not a traditional engagement ring, but it seemed to be made for you."

"It's perfect."

He pulled it out of the box and took her left hand in his. "I love you more than I thought I could love anyone. Will you marry me, Abigail Blue?"

She was sure words couldn't express all the things she was feeling so she simply said, "yes." She let him slide the ring on her finger as she leaned down to kiss him. "I love you, Chase. You're the only diamond I'll ever need."

"I called for an ambulance." The minister came to stand beside Sara and Percy. "It should be at the church soon."

"No ambulance." Chase sat up and took her in his arms. "I have everything I need right here." Then he kissed her like he would never let her go.

Abby thought she heard someone say, "So does this mean we're having a double wedding?" But with her whole world cradled in her arms and the sound of her heart thundering in her ears, she really couldn't be sure.